Rafe

NEW HORIZON RANCH
BOOK 2

DEBRA
CLOPTON

RAFE

Copyright © 2015 Debra Clopton Parks

ABOUT DEBRA CLOPTON

Bestselling author Debra Clopton has sold over 2.5 million books. Her book OPERATION: MARRIED BY CHRISTMAS has been optioned for an ABC Family Movie. Debra is known for her contemporary, western romances, Texas cowboys and feisty heroines. Sweet romance and humor are always intertwined to make readers smile. A sixth generation Texan she lives with her husband on a ranch deep in the heart of Texas. She loves being contacted by readers.

Visit Debra's Website and sign up for her newsletter for news and a chance to win prizes
http://www.debraclopton.com

CONTENTS

CHAPTER ONE

A human-size, fluffy, pink-tailed bunny on the side of the road was the last thing Rafe Masterson expected to see on his way to his brother's engagement party.

He squinted through the sun's rays. "Surely not—" he said, driving closer. But, yup, that was definitely the furry white rump of a bunny bent over the backend of the trunk of the broke down sports car. The critter had a flat tire.

Rafe pressed the brake as the cotton tail wiggled and the bunny popped to a standing position, no bunny head attached. Instead, sun-kissed red hair splayed down the furry back almost touching the cotton tail. Rafe stomped harder on the brake just as Bunny Woman propped one oversized rabbit's foot on the bumper of the car and yanked hard on the spare tire. Instantly it popped free, sending

Bunny Woman and the tire she was clutching stumbling backwards like a drunk on Saturday night.

She tripped over her feet and fell forward on top of the tire, her bunny tail flopping in the breeze just as Rafe barreled from his truck and raced to help. All the while thinking his brother Cliff and his ranch partners weren't going to believe his reason for being late to Cliff's engagement dinner party.

He skidded to a halt just as the redhead rolled off the tire onto her back, bunny feet pointing to the sky by a good eighteen inches. They were huge.

"Are you okay?" He gaped at the massive feet and then the gigantic white belly that sloped to the prettiest, *maddest* bunny he'd ever seen.

"Oh sure," she grunted, magnificent green eyes flashing brilliant as a neon sign. "I'm just peachy wonderful." She struggled to sit up, all the while scowling.

Rafe dropped to one knee and grabbed hold of her fuzzy arm to assist her in her effort. "I hate to break it to you, but you don't look too peachy wonderful to me. You look hotter than a firecracker and a good bit uncomfortable." He held back a chuckle. "I'll fix your tire--"

"Thanks, but no thanks," she snapped.

"Contrary to what it looks like, I can fix my own tire. I thank you for stopping, but I don't need a man to fix my flat." Under her breath, she added, "or anything else."

"Shew, you are miffed about something." He tugged her to her feet without asking if she wanted him to.

"Thanks," she said, then stalked away.

He watched while she clomped toward her car, her feet, thick and long, made splatting sounds on the pavement.

"Hey, hold up," he called, striding to catch her.

She didn't answer. Instead she started digging around inside the trunk, that pink bunny tail flopping sassily with every movement.

Whew, she was mad at someone, and he'd put money on that someone being a man. "I really don't mind helping." He gave her his best grin and placed one hand on rim of the trunk. "It would be a pity for you to get your fur all messed up," he drawled and shot her a smile. "And I hate to mention it, but those feet are probably going to get in your way."

A funny expression on her face, and she looked down at her feet, almost as if she'd forgotten about them. Which is understandable since her belly was so big she couldn't actually *see* her feet. How had she driven the car this far?

She bent forward to see more than her toes. "They roll up—"

"Hand it over, Flossy." Rafe reached for the tire tool. "In Texas when we see a lady or a bunny in distress we stop and help."

Her eyes flashed as his hand wrapped around it. She tugged and held on. He gave her a stern look.

"I'm not gonna stand here and watch you pass out changing that tire--or attempting to change it. From the looks of your cheeks, you won't last long."

"I don't need you," she said.

"Yes, you do." Rafe was known for getting a job done, and he was in serious danger of getting lost in her green eyes and forgetting about everything. "If it helps calm your nerves or anything, I'll introduce myself. I'm Rafe Masterson. I'm part owner of New Horizon Ranch, and I'm well known in Mule Hollow and the surrounding county. You can trust me."

"O-kay." She sighed, looking weary with her pink cheeks and damp skin. "I concede to the cowboy." She let go of the jack. "And thank you."

He grinned. He couldn't help it as he tipped his

hat. "A very smart move. And may I ask your name?"

"Sadie. Sadie Archer"

"Nice to meet you, Sadie."

He turned and set to work, not wanting her to grab hold of the jack again. His mind was racing with questions about Sadie the bunny, but he focused on getting the car jacked up. She moved over to the tire and rolled it in his direction. The fact that she was a large white bunny was still making him want to chuckle, but his curiosity had blown all out of proportion about why in the world she was in the funny getup.

"Are you sure you have time to do this?" she asked, rolling the tire to a stop. "You look like you're all dressed up for a date or something?"

Wondering about her, he'd completely forgotten about Maggie and Cliff's party. "I'm heading to my brother's engagement party. But it'll be fine. I'll call him and let him know I'm running a little late."

She bit her lip and pushed her crimson bangs off her moist forehead.

The sun sizzled here in the middle of Texas at four, even on a mid-September afternoon, and he didn't know how long she'd been out in it before he arrived.

"That suit has to be smothering you. Can't you take it off?"

"Um, no. I can't." She plucked at a piece of lifeless white belly fur. "Believe me, if I could, I would. But I'm fine."

"You don't look fine. You look like you're going to fall over any moment from overheating." He was already damp, and he was only wearing a starched western dress shirt and jeans, no fur. Her cheeks were rapidly turning hot pink.

"I said I was fine."

"Yeah, right." He could look at her and tell that wasn't so. Working fast, he had the flat tire off and the spare in place within a few minutes. The last thing he needed was for her to pass out on him from heat exhaustion. "Done." He let the jack down. "Now, jump inside the car and get some air going to cool those pretty cheeks off."

Looking less perky than she had when he first arrived, she didn't bother to protest. Instead, she trudged over and sank into her seat. That hairy suit had to be getting heavier by the minute. In a moment, he heard the AC blowing full blast. He should have had her sitting in there the whole time, or in his truck. But then as stubborn as she seemed, he figured she probably wouldn't have gotten out of the heat while a complete stranger did work for her.

He dusted off his hands. His job was done, and he had a party to get to, but he didn't feel comfortable leaving her yet. He rested an arm on the top of the door and stared down at her. "Do you need help?"

"You already helped enou--"

"No, I mean are you in trouble?" he asked, gently. "Something doesn't seem right about this situation." And he wasn't one to beat around the bush. He'd been through a lot in his life, and something about her reminded him of the way his mother used to look. Back when he was a kid and home life was hell. Literally. With a no account father she'd protected over and over again, he and his twin brother, Cliff, had been forced to endure a home life that still haunted him in many ways.

He did not take a woman in trouble lightly.

Sadie rubbed her hand on her furry thigh then hesitantly raised her eyes to his. "I'm fine. Do you know if anyone is hiring in Mule Hollow? I could use a job."

Rafe's stomach dipped, and his palms

dampened as he look into those eyes. "Me. I mean our ranch is looking for help."

She studied him, sparks flashing in her eyes. "Seriously, or are you just saying that?"

"No, I'm not," he said too quickly, suddenly for some unexplainable reason wanting her to accept his help. "To be honest, we don't have any need for a five-foot-four-inch bunny, but we could sure use a…a *cook*. Can you cook?"

Her gaze turned probing. Or was that skeptical. "It's not my strong point, but I can manage."

Rafe figured she could have told him she burned toast and scorched eggs and he'd have been fine with that. The fact that she was being honest about her ability was a plus.

"Then you're hired."

Sadie couldn't believe what she was considering. Where had the needing a job bit come from in the first place? Probably because the bunny suit was frying her from the inside out, and the sun was baking her brain.

That and the fact that she still hadn't gotten over the fact that she'd found her fiancé kissing one of her best friends four hours ago.

She closed her eyes and tried to settle the turmoil crashing around inside of her. This had been the worst day of her life, and she'd just complicated it more by mentioning she needed a job. But that was the weird part. She *didn't* need a job, did she? She just needed time. Time to figure out how she'd made such a mess of her life.

She was a strong, independent woman, so how could she have let her relationship with Andrew go this far in the first place?

Because you were tired of waiting while everyone around you got married and had babies.

She sighed, knowing the voice in her heart spoke the truth.

Her stomach churned as she looked up at Rafe Masterson. Why had she mentioned this to him, a total stranger? She should just drive on. "Does being the cook on a ranch come with room and board?" Being a cook on this cowboy's ranch would give her the time she needed to get her thoughts together and figure out what her next move should be.

No one would look for her on a ranch, would they?

She was a city girl, born and bred. And everyone who knew her understood this.

9

No, they'd look for her anywhere but on a cattle ranch.

"Sure it does." The amazingly handsome cowboy stared down at her, and his smoldering gaze dug into her like the tabs on a lie detector machine. Oddly enough, Sadie was tempted to spill her very bad and personal day to the man on the spot.

"Then I'll take the job." She held out her hand to shake on the deal, and he took hers in his larger one. His callused palm sent a jolt of awareness through her. But in its shocking wake, there was also a sense of reassuring strength in his touch. It resonated from his amazing eyes.

"Good," he said, continuing to hold her hand for a moment. "If you want to follow me to the ranch, I'll show you where you'll be working, and I'll introduce you to my other four partners and my brother."

"Sure, that sounds good." What was she doing? The man was chivalrous, good-looking and thoughtful. But still, was she really about to accept a job from a total stranger because her life was in the dumps?

CHAPTER TWO

Evidently she was, Sadie marveled a few minutes later as she followed Rafe through a huge, gorgeous entrance gate. It was made from thick logs and iron work that for some reason relieved and reassured her that he was on the up and up. The drive toward the interior of the ranch was flanked by what seemed like miles of iron pipe fencing separating the driveway from the pretty, rolling pastures that were dotted with black cattle and large oak trees.

When the house came into view, her breath caught. Talk about impressive. It was huge. Gold and tan limestone rock with thick rusty red logs combined to make a substantial house that fit in the setting.

And then she saw the cars. They were everywhere, parked in between the large home and the red barns and buildings that sat several hundred yards from the house. The cars filled the spaces and spilled out along the sides of the driveway next to the house. And then, there were the people.

They stood in groups enjoying the afternoon on the grounds and the huge patio at the back of the house. Obviously a party was going on. She parked beside Rafe, and when he jogged around the end of his truck and opened her car door, she was still gripping her steering wheel as she glared up at him.

"You brought me to a party? I'm wearing a bunny suit." This day had been humiliating on so many levels that had nothing to do with her wearing the bunny suit, but in the aftermath, the suit had made everything else worse. She just wanted out of it.

Rafe hadn't thought about the fact that she was in the bunny suit bothering her. After all, she'd been wearing it on her cross-country drive. Now, looking into her startled eyes, he wasn't sure what she was feeling.

His gut continued to tell him that Sadie was in some kind of trouble, and that was all he'd been thinking about. Now, as he glanced from her to the full parking area between the big house and the barns and stables and the people flowing all across the back of the house, it hit him that he should have given her advance warning.

"I know I mentioned that I was going to an engagement party that three of my partners are throwing for our female partner, Maddie, and my brother. I should have added that it was here on the ranch."

"There are people everywhere," she stated, as if he hadn't by some chance realized this fact.

"Yeah, there are. But it'll be okay. You can change clothes, and I'll introduce you to the good folks of Mule Hollow."

Her expression slid into a perplexed stance. "I don't have any clothes with me."

"Excuse me?"

She shook her head. "When I said I didn't have any clothes on under this thing, I also meant I didn't have any at all. Packed away or anything."

A heatwave rolled over Rafe like drought season in flames. He swallowed. "None?"

She grimaced and shook her head.

"Well." His voice cracked, and he tugged on the starched collar of his shirt. "I mean, how in tarnation did that happen?"

She looked away, and he noticed the vein at the base of her neck was pulsing in overdrive--kind of the way his was pounding at the moment.

"I had to leave town a little unexpectedly." She didn't look at him. Instead her gaze scanned the top of her car back over toward the house and the crowd mingling happily there. She pulled her shoulders back but offered nothing else.

Rafe thought back to the day he and Cliff had struck out from their home. They were twins, though they really just looked like brothers. They'd been seventeen and barely took time to fill plastic bags with a few clothes. He knew what had driven them to leave so quickly, and he couldn't help but wonder what had sent Sadie off without anything but the fur on her back.

Funny, but not funny.

"Someday, I'm gonna have to know the story of how you got stranded inside that confounded bunny suit without--" he paused, trying to think of a gentlemanly way to continue "--without a change of clothes. But right now, we'll figure something out." He glanced toward the yard of people between them and the house. "Tell you what. It might be easier if we went in from the front door instead of the back." He opened the door to his

14

truck. "Slide in here, and I'll drive you closer to the front of the house."

She didn't look at all thrilled by the idea of getting into his truck.

"You can trust me, Sadie. I was hoping you'd figured that out by now. You might not mind if all my friends see you in your suit. I mean, I might be assuming more than I should when I thought you didn't like the idea."

A look of panic came over her. "No, no, you're right. I would rather not be seen in the bunny suit. If at all possible. It's a little humiliating."

Those green eyes of hers sparked like a green flame despite the humiliation in her tone. His lips hitched into a partial grin. "You carry it off well. I figure it'd be all right either way. It's up to you though."

She stood very still for a moment, as if she were considering her options. Then she gave a short nod and climbed inside. He strode around, got in and backed out, all the while wondering what he'd gotten into. What was her story?

Sadie slid a glance at Rafe Masterson, and her stomach dipped again just looking at the gorgeous cowboy. He was tough. That was it. She'd met a lot of good-looking men, and some put on a tough act, some looked tough, and some tried but fell short. There was something about Rafe that told her he'd didn't have to act at being tough. He just was. And there was something inside of her that reacted to that in a very curious and interested way.

And that was just plain dumb on her part.

Ridiculous. Par for the course for her lately though, especially today.

Despite how silly she felt, she knew she was going to have to confess her stupidity. How could she not?

He parked as close to the front of the house as possible, but the circle drive was packed with cars, and so she was still going to have to walk there in her suit.

He had his wrist hanging over the top of the steering wheel, and he cocked his head to look at her. Butterflies like she'd never felt before took flight inside of her. Sitting in the confines of that truck suddenly seemed like they were squeezed together inside a sardine can.

"You ready?" he said, in a concerned drawl that had her nodding quickly and hopping out of the cab like a wolf was after her. She didn't look over her shoulder, just headed toward the front porch of the beautiful home.

A woman in jeans and a blue western shirt came out the front door. "Well, howdy. Aren't you cute in that bunny suit?"

Sadie stopped short and glanced back at Rafe, who'd just caught up with her.

"Hey, Norma Sue." He gave the woman an uncomfortable smile.

A wide, warm smile sprang to the woman's face. She had kinky gray curls that she wore short, making a kind of halo about her head. Not a small woman, she looked sturdy as a tree trunk and capable of anything. Something about the keen assessing eyes told Sadie that Norma Sue was as reliable as she was stout.

"Oh, what a *cute* bunny suit!" A redhead exclaimed, poking her head out the door, big green eyes popping wide as she took Sadie in. "Rafe, a singing telegram is a fun idea, but a bunny for a wedding party? I don't get it?"

"Esther Mae, that wouldn't be the first time you didn't get something," the one named Norma Sue grunted.

"Do *you* get it?" the redhead, Esther Mae, asked her friend indignantly.

17

"Actually, no." Norma Sue looked curiously from Sadie to Rafe.

"It is a cute idea," Esther Mae reiterated, earnestly. "We just don't get it."

Sadie chuckled, and some of the tension she'd been feeling eased a bit. "I'm not a singing telegram ladies, but it is an idea." She didn't know what else to say.

"A very good idea. I'd pay to see it," Rafe said with a grin. "Sadie, I'd like you to meet Norma Sue Jenkins and Esther Mae Wilcox. This is Sadie. She had a flat tire."

Both ladies greeted her, then Esther Mae arched a pale eyebrow. "Why do you have the suit on? I can't help it. I'm curious."

"I was just dressed up for visiting some of the children at Texas Children's Hospital."

"Oh! Isn't that nice," Esther Mae exclaimed. "Norma, that's better than a singing telegram, don't you think?"

"It's wonderful," Norma Sue said at the same time.

Rafe placed his hand at the small of her back, and she looked up at him. His expression was gentle as their gazes met. He smiled approvingly at her. "Ladies, if you'll excuse us, I'm going to take

Sadie in and show her where she can change. She's probably hot and ready to get out of that suit."

Esther Mae looked sympathetic. "I bet it's itchy. It's cute and all, but I'd suffocate in there."

"Come on out and see us when you get changed," Norma Sue said and hustled her friend off the front porch. "Rafe, we were just admiring the house. It's been a long time since we've been out here. That C.C., God rest his soul, didn't invite many folks out here when he was in town. I think he liked to just enjoy the peace and quiet when he wasn't living his high powered corporate lawyer job."

"He sure did have good taste," Esther Mae quipped. "This is a showplace, and that's for certain. Rafe, you and your partners have kept it up nice since he died and left it to y'all."

"Yes, ma'am, we try to keep things like C.C. liked them. He willed it to us, but he did it because he knew we each loved the place as much as he did. He felt like we could make a profit and keep his legacy going. But also, he was just that kind of man."

Norma Sue's expression was thoughtful. "He chose well. You five really know your stuff." She looked at Sadie. "This here is a fine, smart cattleman."

Sadie glanced at Rafe and noticed an odd, almost suspicious look come over his expression.

"It's true," Esther Mae assured her. "And handsome too." Her green eyes twinkled as they moved from Rafe to Sadie.

"Thank you. I'm sure y'all are wanting to get back to the party," he said, and held the door open for Sadie. "After you."

She didn't need any encouragement. "I'm sure I'll see you ladies later. It was nice to meet you both." Before they had time to reply, Rafe had the door closed behind them and was ushering her down the hall. She got the distinct impression that something was bothering him, but she didn't ask. Instead, she took in the large room they entered right off the entrance hall. It was huge with high ceilings that rose two stories and had a staircase that curved up to the second level. The furnishings were large and masculine. With its wood floors, colorful throw rugs, Texas flavored furnishings of unique wooden tables and chairs, the place reminded her of photo layouts she'd seen in many different magazines of a top-notch hunting lodges.

She could hear people talking in another room, which was connected to the one they were. She assumed it was the kitchen. Rafe started up the stairs, and she followed, relieved she wasn't going to meet others at the moment. Her feet flopped on the stairs, and she tried to step lightly, hoping not to make too much noise. The bunny suit had begun to feel as if she were carrying a full grown black bear on her shoulders, and she was anxious to tear it off. She had no idea what she was going to do for clothes, but felt certain that Rafe had something in mind. All she could do was trust him.

"Where are we going?" she asked quietly. It came out more of a hiss as she tried not to be heard, really hoping they would make it up the stairs before anyone else spotted them.

"I'm taking you to one of the guest rooms, and then I'll go get Maddie. She'll have something for you to wear, I'm certain."

She'd been right. He had it under control. Rafe Masterson struck her as the kind of guy who always had everything under control. They made it to the landing without mishap.

Suddenly one of the doors on the top floor opened, and two cowboys came walking out. They both stopped short at the sight of her.

Like Rafe, both looked to be in their late twenties, early thirties, and they were dressed similarly to him in starched western shirts and jeans, with the look was finished off by boots and hats. It was enough to make a gal who'd sworn off men reconsider her decision. One had light brown hair, a wide jaw and serious gray eyes. The other reminded her of Blake Shelton, with dark wavy hair and olive green eyes that lit up with the smile that slammed across his face when he saw her.

"Rafe," he drawled, sweeping his hat from his head. "Who've you got with you?"

The other man had removed his hat too, but looked on expectantly not saying anything. Instead, he waited for Rafe to answer.

"Ah, Dalton," Rafe said, addressing the Blake lookalike and then the other. "Ty, y'all, this is Sadie. She had a little car trouble, and I'm showing her to an extra room so she can change clothes."

Dalton grinned bigger. "I'm glad to meet you, ma'am," he drawled again, with the manners of a Texas charmer who *probably* did his fair share of flirting and laying it on thick when he wanted to.

"If y'all will excuse us, I'll catch y'all downstairs. Would one of you go find Maddie and ask her to come up here?"

"Sure, whatever you want," Dalton said.

The quieter one nodded. "Nice to meet you. See

you downstairs, Rafe."

They moved on, and when Rafe opened a door, Sadie was never so happy to see a bedroom in all of her life.

"I'll wait downstairs and send Maddie up as soon as she comes in and grabs you some things to wear. Is there anything I can get you? There's a bathroom connected to the room, but you might want to look and see if it's got everything you need. You know, if you want to freshen up or something."

He suddenly looked uncomfortable and out of his element.

"If there's a towel and soap, then I'd love to go ahead and take a shower. This thing is like wearing fiberglass insulation."

"Go ahead. All that's in there. I'll tell Maddie you might be in the shower when she gets here with the clothes."

"Okay. She could just leave them on the bed." Sadie had reached her limit. Not only did she need to get out of the itchy suit, she needed a bathroom break in the worst way.

"Then enjoy your shower, and I'll see you when you're done." With that, he turned and headed back down the stairs.

Sadie started yanking at Velcro the instant the door closed. She hurried to the bathroom as she tugged and pulled and maneuvered out of the suit. Cool air hit her hot, irritated skin, and relief surged over her. Within moments, she was in the walk-in shower in the gorgeous bathroom. As she let the hot water pour over her, she wondered again, what she was doing?

CHAPTER THREE

Maddie had just come inside when Rafe reached the kitchen. She looked pretty in her dressy jeans and soft pink top. She was as tough as he, Chase, Ty and Dalton, but a whole lot prettier. Today she didn't look like the tough cowgirl he knew, but instead a sweet gal who was soon to be his sister-in-law.

"What's this I hear about you having a bunny in here?" Her blue eyes were filled with curiosity.

Before he could get a word out, Ty, Chase and Dalton and his brother, Cliff, crowded into the kitchen behind her asking questions.

"Okay, y'all, here's the deal. I found Sadie stranded on the side of the road with a flat tire and wearing a bunny suit. That's all I know. Except that she needed help, kinda looked like she was in some kind of trouble, so…I've hired her on as the cook."

Five sets of eyes stared back at him as if he were an alien or something.

"The cook," Maddie said first.

"Well, yeah, with you going to be over at your own house and the way we are always scrounging around, I figured it might be a good thing."

Chase, who was the one who kept the books and wrote the checks for all their hired hands, looked thoughtful for a moment, then hiked a shoulder. "I think it's a good idea, but do you know anything about her?"

"I hadn't gotten that far."

Cliff grinned. "Nope. My brother saw a woman who needed help, and he offered it."

"Y'all would have done the same thing," Rafe said, knowing it was true, but glad it had been him. "Okay, y'all get back out there to the BBQ. I don't want her to come downstairs and find everyone gawking. I need to talk to Maddie. I'll bring her out to meet y'all in just a bit."

"So, what's up?" Maddie asked after the others left.

"Well, there's something else I didn't mention. She doesn't have any clothes."

Maddie's eyes got wide. "None?"

"She's taking a shower. Do you think you could

26

find a few things for her? She's about your size."

"Sure I can. I'll handle this. You go on outside. So you have no idea what's going on?"

"None. But I will. Thanks, Maddie. I hate to do this at your engagement party."

"Hey, not a problem. Go on now. I've got this. Is she in the guest room?"

"Yes. Thanks again," he said, relieved to hand it over to Maddie.

"Stop looking so worried, Rafe. I'll take good care of her." Maddie studied him. "You like her." It wasn't a question. "I think that's great."

"Don't go to jumping to any conclusions. I just met her, and there's more unanswered questions than there are answered."

"True, but the key is you're interested in finding out the answers to those questions."

And she was right.

When a knock sounded on the door, Sadie poked her head out. Wrapped in a towel, she wasn't sure who would be standing there.

"Hi, Sadie. I'm Maddie Rose, and I'm here with clothes," said the pretty, dark-headed woman about Sadie's age.

27

"Please come in." She stepped back and opened the door. Maddie carried an armful of clothes with her and even some shoes.

"*Shoes.*, I hadn't even thought of those. You probably think I'm awful."

"Naw, I figure you've got a very good reason to be stranded without clothes. I have to say I'm not at all sure why you'd be wearing a bunny suit, which, I might add, I need to see to believe." Maddie's eyes twinkled as she laid the clothes on the bed.

Relief washed over Sadie as she realized Maddie might be someone she could relate to. She seemed down to earth and practical. A what-you-see-is-what-you-get kind of gal. Sadie needed that. She'd felt so betrayed at finding Andrew, her fiancé, with his secretary. She was still reeling from that, almost more than Andrew's betrayal.

"It's a long story, and I'll fill you in later. You're missing your engagement party."

"We'll get there. First I'm helping you. Mule Hollow folks don't rush parties. They'll hang around, and we'll all have time to enjoy ourselves. I wasn't sure what would work, so I brought a variety of things from jeans to stretchy stuff. There's some underthings too."

Sadie stared at the clothes and suddenly felt blessed in the midst of this horrible day.

From the moment Rafe had stopped to help her, it had been that way. A lump formed in her throat. "Thank you," she managed softly, then picked up a blouse.

They spent the next few minutes going through the items, and Sadie actually was the same size as Maddie. Another blessing. She was, however, a little taller. But thankfully, several of the things worked perfectly.

Sadie hurried, not wanting to keep Maddie from her guests too long and knowing the quicker she dressed, the sooner they could get to the party.

Hurrying and trying to focus on the blessings of this horrible day, Sadie couldn't completely sideline thoughts of her own party she wasn't showing up for back home. Anger rushed hot and coarse through her, but at the same time, relief steadied her. She had known something wasn't right. Had known she was making a mistake.

So why did it still hurt so much?

"Seriously? She was wearing a bunny suit?"

At Chase's question, Rafe grinned, despite

knowing Ty and Dalton were studying him. They were still unable to believe the getup she'd been wearing or that he'd hired her on the spot. "Yes, one of those kind you see someone wear to a kid's birthday party."

"I bet that was a shocker," Ty said.

"Pretty much." Rafe still felt a bit of that shock.

Dalton grinned. "I'm just glad we have a cook. Man, oh, man, that's gonna be nice."

Grins spread across their faces. They normally took turns with cooking duties, but they got up early and worked late a lot, and so their meals were nothing to celebrate.

They were standing to the side watching the main throng heading toward the fajita line of the party that was now in full swing. When they'd come back outside, Cliff had immediately been surrounded by well-wishers and his admiring group of young cowboys who were always after him for tips to help their own bull riding endeavors.

Rafe still couldn't believe his bull riding champion of a brother had come to town and, in a whirlwind romance with Maddie that had lasted less than two weeks, had fallen in love and asked Maddie to marry him. It was crazy. As far as Rafe was concerned, it was reckless. But it wasn't for him to say one way or the other. As long as they were happy, that was all that mattered. Cliff deserved to be happy, and Rafe was glad he'd finally been able to leave the demons of their past behind and stop running. Rafe had stopped running a long time ago, and though he had a good life, he knew deep inside, he still dealt with the past in many ways.

He was glad Cliff and Maddie both had found love. Still, two weeks was a little fast for Rafe. He was more cautious than that, and with reason.

"So how long do you give them?" Ty asked, looking worried. Rafe was glad the conversation was shifted from him and Sadie.

He shrugged. "I'm going to give them forever. I know my brother. Once he commits to something, wind from a hurricane couldn't shake him loose. And you've seen the poor sodbuster when Maddie's around. He's about as love-struck as a man could be."

"I agree," Chase added. "I just hope he really loves Maddie. She deserves it."

"Yeah," Dalton grunted. "She does."

"He better not let her down. That's all I have to say," Ty said quietly. He didn't say much, but he meant what he said. And he had a soft spot for

Maddie just like the rest of them.

Ever since she'd come to the ranch and begun working beside them two years ago, she'd been tough and tougher. She just wouldn't stop. And there was no way you could miss that she loved what she did. Hard or not, she loved it. That was one reason they all felt like C.C., their boss, had included them all in his will, leaving them equal partners in the ranch. They all loved the ranch and the work. C.C. had loved it too, and since he had no children, he'd left it to all of them. It was something none of them had expected or had completely gotten used to. Maddie especially.

"Okay, now, back to the bunny." Chase cocked his head. "You know with a new female in town, the Posse is going to be on high alert."

Rafe and all the others made several various grunts of agreement on that. The Matchmakin' Posse would eat this up. His gaze slid across the yard to Norma Sue, Esther Mae and the petite Adela Ledbetter Green. The three older women wore their nicknames proudly after starting an ad campaign years earlier to save the town by advertising for wives for the local cowboys. The town was thriving because of their matchmaking efforts. They'd played both small and large parts in matching up most of the couples standing around the lawn right now. Including Cliff and Maddie.

Dalton cocked his head. "You better be watching your back if they get wind of you rescuing the bunny, or you'll end up like your brother."

Hitching a brow, Rafe frowned. "I think they've figured out I'm not a good prospect."

Everyone chuckled, and Chase just shook his head. "Most of the cowboys who are married off now weren't lookin' either. They still got matched up and married off."

Rafe's neck suddenly started itching just thinking about it. He hoped that, just because he'd helped Sadie, they didn't get interested in him. He'd flown under the radar for a while now, and he had his reasons to stay there.

He glanced toward the patio door, unable to halt the anticipation seeing of Sadie walking out in something other than the infamous bunny suit.

That in no way meant he was planning on jumping off into a romance with her. An elbow caught him in the side.

"Earth to partner," Chase said.

"Sorry." Rafe grunted, seeing his other partners grinning. He scowled. "Aren't y'all hungry yet?"

"No need to get testy," Dalton drawled. "We're

going."

Ty glanced from Rafe back to the door. "Yup. Fajita line's calling our name," he said, then sauntered off with a chuckle.

Chase tucked his fingers in his pockets and eyed him hard. "Just between you and me, you look kind of like you've been struck by lightning."

"What's that supposed to mean?"

"Don't bite my head off. It's just an observation. Because you might be here in body, but your mind never arrived."

A throb started behind Rafe's eyes. "Okay, so yeah, I think she's something. But don't go yacking to everyone about it. The last thing I want is to stir up the pot with the Posse."

"Do you really think I'd go and do something like that to you?"

Rafe did not like the glint in Chase's eyes. "Yeah, I do. Just because you think this is so funny." Chase's grin widened, and Rafe scowled harder. "I'm warning you, Chase, no matchmakers."

"Okay, okay. I'm just kidding. You don't go having a heart attack or something. For your information, I'm staying out of it, because I don't intend to draw any attention to myself. So you can stop worrying."

"That's more like it…" Rafe's words trailed off as the patio door opened. Every muscle in his body tensed. Maddie walked out first, and his heart thumped madly in his chest. His body hummed, as if he'd just ridden a fast horse across an arena. Nothing had ever given him the rush he'd felt when he'd competed in steer roping. Nothing until the instant Sadie walked out of that door.

His thundering heart stumbled. *Wow.*

The thumping regained its rhythm and galloped onward. He couldn't move. She'd been something in a bunny suit, but now, wow. Holy cow, he was in trouble.

The last time he'd felt that way was over six years ago when he'd fallen in love with a girl who— he shoved thoughts of Dawn from his mind. This was not the time or the place to let old memories sideswipe him. He wasn't sure why his ex-fiancée had suddenly started rolling through his mind. It wasn't as if he'd spent the last three years mourning the fact that she'd dropped him and walked out of his life the night his NFR dreams had died.

No, it had been the opposite. When he'd jumped from his horse and destroyed his knee and any chance at the championship, Dawn had bolted.

He'd wiped her from his mind after a few weeks of feeling sorry for himself, but it still disgusted him to think back to how badly her leaving had affected him. He hated thinking about it, about how weak he'd felt. He'd felt weak and helpless as a kid up against his dad beating his mother, and it was a feeling Rafe couldn't stand. He'd gone through it twice in his life, and he didn't plan on ever going through it again.

It was evidently left over from when he was growing up.

Instead of mourning the loss, he'd banned thoughts of Dawn from his mind.

But now she suddenly kept popping into his thoughts, and all because Sadie hit a cord inside him that ran deep.

Maddie headed over to join Cliff and the group he was talking with while Sadie crossed the grass to him.

"I feel so much better," she said, eyes sparkling. "Maddie was great, and I'm grateful we're about the same size."

"Yeah, that was a lucky break or you'd have been wearing my clothes." The moment he thought about her putting on his shirt, his entire body flushed with heat.

Okay, back up, Hoss. Way up.

She was standing close enough that the fresh, sweet scent of her filled his senses. Flowers and spring time. He fought the urge to lean in and breathe his fill of her. As if she felt the tug of awareness too, she stared at him with huge green eyes as the moment stretched into two. She would think he had lost his mind if he traced the curve of her cheek with his fingertips and then tilted her chin up and kissed her. Nope. Not happening. And certainly not here in front of God and everyone. Including the Matchmakin' Posse. He glanced over and sure enough caught Esther Mae watching them with a speculative eye. He stiffened and tried to look less interested in Sadie. Which was hard to do when this woman he'd just met had him feeling like a skinny kid with his first crush.

"Maddie said everyone was excited that you hired a cook."

"Um, yeah, they are. They're cowboys. Cooking isn't our top priority, but eating ranks *real* high. You're going to be one popular lady. Speaking of that, prepare yourself. The stampede is coming."

"What?" she said, and he nodded behind her.

Chase, Cliff and Maddie were making their way over across the yard. As were several others. Lacy and Clint Matlock, Dottie and Brady Cannon, and the three worrisome ladies responsible for "fixin'" the two couples up and marrying them off. There was a glint of joy in the ladies' eyes. He was in trouble.

Big trouble.

And he'd walked straight into their sights like his head was stuffed with feathers…or bunny fluff…instead of a brain.

Yup, bunny fluff…that was exactly what had just put him in hot water.

CHAPTER FOUR

Chase was the partner she'd not met, and he was the first to reach them. A handsome man with serious eyes but a ready smile.

"Glad to meet you," he said. "Also glad Rafe happened upon you. This was too hot of a day to be stranded on the side of the road. Looks like we have company," he said and winked. "You are officially the talk of the town."

After that, Sadie met more people, whose names she would never be able to remember. There were couples of all ages and cowboys without wives of varying ages, too. Norma Sue and Esther Mae introduced her to their other friend, Adela. She was a tiny, almost fragile-looking lady with a snow white cap of hair framing amazing blue eyes that seemed to read Sadie's very soul. Sadie would have no trouble remembering her name.

"I believe you've got a treat in store for yourself working at this ranch," she said, taking Sadie's hands in her finely boned hands. "These are a fine bunch of young men and a wonderful lady you'll be working with."

"I told her the same thing about this rowdy bunch," Maddie said. "I'm glad to have another female around."

Then she met Maddie's fiancé, Cliff, who was supposed to be Rafe's twin. But there was only enough resemblance for them to be brothers, so she assumed they seldom got pinned as twins. Cliff held Maddie around the waist and shook Sadie's hand with his other hand. He was recognizably smitten by Maddie, and Sadie felt a twinge of regret for what she and Andrew had not had.

Before she could get too morose, she was introduced to more people from Mule Hollow. Lacy and Clint Matlock. Lacy co-owned the hair salon in town, and Clint owned a large ranch. Lacy was pregnant with their second child. Sadie felt that familiar ache of baby envy as she shook Lacy's hand. She was twenty-eight years old and wanted a baby so badly that it had driven her to irrationally accept Andrew's marriage proposal. That mistake topped the list of mistakes she could see now.

"We are so excited about the baby." Lacy beamed. She had a wild head of wavy blonde hair that hung just above her shoulders.

Clint was in his mid-thirties and really looked like a great guy. The way he was looking proudly and lovingly at Lacy sent another ache through Sadie.

Okay, she was a little sentimental tonight…and with good reason.

She didn't get more than a first impression of the couple, though, as she was introduced to Dottie and Brady Cannon. Brady was the sheriff, and he and his wife also owned and operated a shelter for abused women that they housed in a home on their ranch. They too looked so happy together.

"We were wondering—" Norma Sue broke into the introductions "—if you ever did something for the kiddos at shelters like No Place Like Home on Dottie and Brady's place? We thought if you visited little sick kids in hospitals that you just might visit little kids who are hurting emotionally at shelters."

Sadie's heart leapt. "*Yes*, I love doing that. You really have a shelter here in this small town?" she asked Dottie. Her want of her own children fueled her love of all children and the need to reach out and help them in some way. Thus, the bunny ministry.

"Yes, it's a long story of how it got here. But it's true. We help a lot of ladies and their children find safety and a fresh start. We'd love to have you come out."

"I will. After I get settled, we'll set something up."

And after that, it was a whirlwind of introductions. She tried hard to remember names, but part of the problem was she was acutely aware of Rafe standing to the side, and she couldn't deny the draw between them.

She was also well aware that in an hour she was supposed to be at her own engagement party back at the country club, with her parents presiding over everything with bold authority, proud that their daughter was making such a match.

Her stomach knotted, and she forced her thoughts back to the conversation.

"That will be awesome that you'll come out as a bunny," Lacy said. "You'll get a blessing out of it. I guarantee it. Dottie does an amazing job out there. And she also owns the candy store in town where the women can work and learn about how to run their own businesses. You'd be amazed at how many women she's given new starts just through empowering them with new skills."

"Really. That is so neat." Sadie was very intrigued and for a moment forgot her other worries.

"Sadie," Esther Mae said, her gaze flitting to Sadie's left hand. "I don't see a ring on your finger, so I'm assuming you're single. Is there someone special back home?"

Sadie coughed, choked. "N-no, ma'am." Everyone was looking at her. Some of the husbands chuckled. Lacy smiled, shook her head and started to say something, but Rafe broke in.

"I think it's time to get something to eat," he said, placing his hand at the small of her back. "Aren't you hungry?"

His touch was warm, and she was extremely aware of it, but she knew it was because she was so startled by Esther Mae's question. She hadn't been ready for that. "I am, actually. It's been a while since…lunch." She almost said since breakfast, which was true, but she didn't want to bring more uncomfortable questions her way on why she hadn't eaten.

Sadie didn't miss the looks exchanged between the three friends as Norma Sue waved toward the food. "Y'all go on over there and grab some of

Sam's good food. And sit over there under that big oak. Sadie probably needs all the shade she can get after being stuck in this sun all afternoon."

Sadie glanced from one smiling older lady to the other before Lacy's chuckle drew her attention.

"Enjoy," she urged. "And we'll talk more later. Maybe over coffee or lunch at the diner one day this week."

"Yes, that will be fun," Dottie agreed. "Go eat right now." She glanced from Sadie to the three beaming older ladies and shook her head slightly with a twitch of her lips.

Odd. Very odd. Sadie was missing something here, and she knew it as she headed off with Rafe.

It was obvious that the ladies were really glad she and Rafe were eating together. And it was obvious that Lacy. and Dottie found something slightly amusing.

But what? Her stomach grumbled, reminding her she was starving.

"The fajitas look great," Rafe said, stopping at the long table and picking up a plate and handing it to her.

They looked delicious, and the scent was mouthwatering. Sadie's stomach growled loudly.

"Whoa," Rafe said, looking more alarmed than

he had when Esther Mae asked the boyfriend question. "It's really time I fed you."

Embarrassment singed her cheeks. "I'm sorry. I haven't eaten for a little while. I didn't stop for lunch and then had the flat and, well, a growling stomach is what I get."

"Make sure you get as much as you want. Sam catered this, and there is no one around who knows food like Sam Green. There he is over there busy as a bee. The man is small but has the energy of about twenty people." He pointed out a small man who was hustling about at the end of the table and overseeing some servers as he added new meat to the trays. "I'll introduce you when we get down there. You doing okay, other than being hungry?"

"I'm fine. Everyone is so welcoming." She didn't mention the odd looks she'd seen exchanged between the older ladies. Instead, she began loading her plate. She didn't go overboard, but she could have easily done so with the beef and chicken and the onions and green peppers and much more that were set out across the table.

She thought of the delicate meal her mother had carefully ordered for her dinner that night, and she almost lost her appetite. She should have called. Mom would say it was in very bad taste not to. As

45

if on cue, her phone vibrated in her pocket. She'd not only had the shock of her life today, but she'd become a chicken.

Rafe introduced her to Sam, a very nice man, and then they headed to the table beneath a large oak tree, the one Norma Sue had suggested.

"I need to return a phone call, but I'll be right back," she told Rafe as she set her plate down.

"Sure. I'll go grab us some tea and meet you back here."

She nodded and then walked a little away from everything before sliding the phone from her pocket.

Her mother had called twice. Somehow she'd been so distracted that she hadn't even felt the vibration on one of her calls.

Andrew had called several times earlier, but he was no longer calling. Hopefully he'd gotten the message that she wasn't ready to talk to him, the lying cheat.

But she did need to talk to her mother, needed to tell her what had happened. But it was complicated. Her mother really had her heart set on Andrew being Sadie's husband. After losing Dad two years ago, this wedding seemed to have put a spark back in Mom's eye. And there was also the fact that her mother had a very strong personality when she really wanted something. This wedding had brought that out. But with Andrew, she'd stepped over a boundary and had taken over everything…and Sadie had let her. She knew it. Had told herself over and over again she needed to pull her mother back, but she hadn't. She had told herself she loved Andrew and wanted a baby so badly, and somehow she'd just let everything snowball.

Once she'd accepted the proposal and her mother had taken over, the wedding planning had taken on a life of its own. Her plans for a year-long engagement had shrunk to three months, and Sadie had immediately started to panic internally. Questioning her own motives had been her first point of worry, but then she'd started to see Andrew's motives too.

All the while her mother had happily ramrodded the wedding planning.

Unease burned in her stomach as she pushed the button and waited for her mother to answer.

"Where are you? Guests are starting to arrive, and I have no daughter here."

"And hello to you too, Mom." Sadie was startled at her tone and her lack of apparent concern. Sadie could have been stranded on the side of the road with a flat tire or something.

"I'm past hello, young lady. Andrew is here, and he's asking where you are, too. He said he hasn't spoken to you all day and that you haven't returned his calls."

He what? Sadie really couldn't believe the louse had even shown up at the party and was leading her mother to think there wasn't anything wrong.

"I'm sorry, Mother. I'm…I'm not--" she hedged, shocked. "--coming." Hurt stung deep that her mother hadn't asked if she was hurt, hadn't even sounded worried. Did this marriage mean so much to her that she wasn't concerned for Sadie?

Her stomach rolled at the thought.

There was only silence on the other end of the line. "What exactly does that mean?" her mother finally asked, her tone softening. "Sadie, are you all right?"

Tears welled up in Sadie's eyes. A little late to ask, but at least she had finally realized something could be wrong.

"I should have called earlier. The wedding is off."

"Young lady, you listen to me. You only have cold feet. I don't know where you are. But I expect you here within minutes. Cold feet are common. This is not acceptable."

So much for her concern. "Not acceptable?" Sadie's stomach knotted. Despite her shock at her mother's choice of words, she'd actually, subconsciously known this would be her reaction. Maybe that was why Sadie hadn't stopped driving until she'd blown a tire. She was far enough away now that she couldn't make it back to the party even if she wanted to. And she didn't want to.

"Mother," she said, trying to make her voice sound sympathetic to the position she'd placed her mother in. "There are things you don't understand. Andrew is having an affair. But I--"

"Sadie, he is an up-and-coming powerhouse. He is going places, and men like that are under tremendous pressure. They-they are expected to have needs."

"Excuse me?" Sadie couldn't believe this. "Mother, I can't believe you'd say such a thing. There is no excuse for his behavior." Trembling from anger and shock, Sadie ended the call, her head spun from fury and frustration swirling around inside of her. A chill flashed over her as she stuffed the phone in her pocket and blinked away tears.

She'd never felt so alone in all of her life.

CHAPTER FIVE

"Is everything all right?"

Rafe had come back to the table and sat down with his and Sadie's iced tea. He'd watched her as she spoke on the phone. She looked distressed. Her expression and her stance as every muscle in her body appeared to tense. After she was finished, she looked more distressed, and she didn't immediately turn and come his way. She was regaining her composure.

Rafe tensed, wondering what was driving Sadie. What was she hiding from or running from? He wanted to ask her, but he didn't want to scare her off before she'd had a chance to settle in.

She sank into the chair and picked up the glass of tea and took a drink, as if to give herself more time to think. He took a drink of his and waited.

"Thanks for this," she said, drumming her

fingertips on the table. Her expression was tense. "Everything will be okay."

Rafe was pretty sure the brightness in her eyes was unshed tears. But were they from sadness or anger?

She didn't look like everything would be okay. Rafe understood better than most that sometimes a person needed to deal with things in their own way in their own time. But he didn't feel right not asking what was wrong.

"This seems like a really nice group of people," she said, gathering the edges of her flour tortilla so the chicken and green peppers and other fixin's were gathered up inside it. "Have you lived here all of your life?"

Nope, he didn't like not asking about her situation, but he went along with it for now. "They're real nice. I've lived here for a little more than six years. I started working on the ranch after I got injured and had to stop competing in the rodeo."

"Oh, I'm sorry you got hurt. What did you do in the rodeo?"

"Tie-down roping."

"That's where you chase the calf, rope it and throw yourself off the horse at a run, then flip the calf and tie him, right?"

"Right." He chuckled. "I have to say that I wasn't expecting you to know that."

"Hey, most Texans know a little about rodeo. But--" she held up a hand "--I will admit that I don't know a lot."

A very cute smile played across her pretty lips, making Rafe want to see her do that more often. "In that case, you're in the right zip code. I can assure you of that." They just stared at each other for a moment, and Rafe was suddenly uncomfortable. He'd just met Sadie, and she'd already gotten under his skin. That was a very hard thing to do these days.

"So you hurt yourself? How?" she asked, tilting her head slightly, her tawny hair falling over her shoulder.

He didn't talk about his past much. Especially this. Most people who knew him knew he'd been a competitor, and his brother and partners knew about his blown career. But he didn't talk about it much. "Hurt my knee. You have to have your knees in that event." He had gotten used to saying that without revealing how deeply he'd struggled with the decision that had changed his life. He'd made peace with it, but it had taken his moving to

Mule Hollow before that had happened.

Her eyes softened. "That was really hard on you, wasn't it?"

It wasn't a question, and the fact that she seemed to know it was hard for him drew him to her more. He nodded. "It was. You better eat that fajita before it gets cold, or you'll miss out on a Mule Hollow treasure. Sam knows how to make one mean fajita."

She chuckled. "Is it going to hurt me?"

"No, ma'am. It's going to make your day."

"Boy, do I need that," she said, and lifted the filled tortilla and took a bite. Her eyes widened as she chewed. "Oh my," she mumbled, then continuing to chew she nodded.

"Told you." He smiled, then took a bite of his own fajita.

After that they ate in silence for a contented moment. And all the while, he wondered what the phone call had been about.

The music started up while they were eating, and Maddie and Cliff moved to the dance area.

Cliff smiled at Maddie and took her in his arms. Rafe watched as a deep satisfaction filled him for his brother and for Maddie. They'd found what he hadn't been able to find, but he was thrilled for them.

Glancing back at Sadie, he saw that troubled look shadow her expression.

"You want to talk about it yet?"

She shook her head. "No, I don't."

"Then I'm thinking a dance might be in order to celebrate the fact that you aren't still sitting on the side of the road impersonating a carrot loving cottontail and that New Horizon Ranch has just scored a win with a fantastic, amazing new cook."

She laughed, startling herself, if the shocked look in her eyes was any indication of her feelings. "Wait, hold on. I told you I could cook okay, but far from fantastic and amazing."

"And I wasn't talking about your cooking. I was talking about the cook." He stood and held out his hand. "Shall we?"

She nodded slowly and slipped her hand in his. He pulled her close. Not as close as he suddenly wanted to, but close enough that he could smell the sweet scent of her. And then he had to fight off the urge to pull her fully into his arms…

Sadie had had the worst day of her life, and she was now dancing in Rafe's arms…and smiling! She couldn't believe it. Shouldn't she feel horrible? Of course she should, but instead, butterflies were winging their way through her as he pulled her within the security of his arms. Her heart pounded at his nearness, and she didn't feel alone against the world as she had moments ago. George Straight sang over the speakers, but she barely heard him as her thoughts were consumed with her cowboy in shining armor. The man not only made butterflies go crazy inside of her, but there was something about the way he held her and the way he looked at her with those steady eyes that made her feel everything was going to be all right as long as he was holding her. And she needed that.

It helped her feel steady after talking with her mother. It helped her hold strong, and she needed that.

It also helped her realize that everything she'd been feeling about not marrying Andrew was right.

But most of all, when she looked up at Rafe, she felt like she'd just stepped into a fairytale. It wouldn't last, but just for right now, she'd take what she could get, because she'd never, ever felt like this before.

Sadie sat by the window and worried long after the party was over and she'd gone to her room. Long after Rafe had asked her once more if she was okay--to which she'd told him she would be fine. She wasn't.

Her phone was full of texts from friends and family wondering what had happened. Wanting to know how she was. Andrew also resumed calling and leaving messages, which she did not answer or even listen to. Yes, she would have to deal with everything, but not right now. She was too angry. Too hurt...too confused. Confused with her feelings and emotions most of all.

Despite knowing that in the morning she would face the cooking problem, she was so thankful for the distraction that Rafe and this job were giving her. She hadn't lied about not being a great cook. She could make coffee and use a microwave, but to actually cook something was another story. She'd never really had to cook before. Until she'd moved out on her own, Ms. Wriggly, her mother's cook/housekeeper, had taken her job seriously. Since moving out on her own Sadie had never had the urge or desire to up her skills, and thus she tended to eat out a lot or just warmed something up. She could cook a few simple things, but breakfast was not one of those things. Rafe was willing to hire her, so she was willing to give it her best shot. The distraction was more than welcomed.

Thankfully, Rafe had said he'd meet her in the kitchen at six a.m. to help her and show her around the kitchen. The idea of seeing him again was the bright spot in her thoughts. She tried hard not to think too badly of herself for thinking such a thing. As a matter of fact, the fact that she did find him so attractive showed that even before knowing Andrew was an unfaithful roach of a man, she'd known she couldn't go through with the wedding. Known settling for someone she'd thought she loved was not ever going to make up for giving up on finding the man who would make her heart ache with love for him. And the fact that she was so quickly attracted to Rafe was positive affirmation that she could and would wait for the right man before she ever acted so foolishly again. She just had to make herself not think about whether the man of her heart was out there and that he might not show up.

No, she wouldn't think about that. Rafe was dulling that thought anyway. The man was gorgeous and had enough charisma for five men piled into that fabulous body of his. The way he smiled caused her internal compass to spin in a dizzying whirlwind that she'd never experienced before. So, was this simply from the strain of yesterday?

She was in no emotional state of mind to trust anything she was feeling right now.

However, when she finally drifted off to sleep sometime in the early hours this morning, it was with thoughts of Rafe coming to her rescue on the side of the road. And she realized that instead of curling up and crying over the traumatic day, she found herself smiling as she went to sleep. The cowboy must have thought he was seeing things when he saw her in her bunny suit rolling around with that tire. She was thankful he hadn't thought she was a crazy person and kept on driving.

The truth was that Rafe might well be the saving grace who was going to keep her from going insane through this wedding meltdown she was having.

CHAPTER SIX

"Good morning."

Sadie jumped at the slow drawl as she entered the kitchen at about five forty-five the next morning. Rafe, looking perfect in older jeans and a dark T-shirt and boots, was leaning against the counter beside the coffee pot. He held a mug up.

"Would you like a cup?"

"I'd give my pinky toe for one, thank you. You sure are up early."

He chuckled, a deep, rich sound that pooled inside her.

"No need to cut off body parts. I'm sure that pinky toe is too cute to lose, so hold on a minute while I pour you a cup. And I wouldn't have had you start your first morning alone no matter what. But on the ranch, we always start our mornings early. Best part of the day."

"We might have to disagree about that last part." She took the mug he handed her and smelled the eye popping delicious scent of the coffee. Just the scent helped clear her thoughts. "This is so needed. Thanks for coming down on my first morning. I need you."

Their gazes locked up on that, and they both took cautious sips of the steaming brew.

"Get a few sips of that in you, and then we'll get started."

She wasn't going to argue about that. The strong, caustic goodness seeped through her like a jolt of lightening. She was thankful for the adrenaline surge caused by facing something new. It helped her not be as exhausted as she should have been because of the night she'd had and, of course, the emotions of yesterday.

Instantly the thought crept in. *A week from today would have been my wedding day. What if I hadn't decided to break off the engagement? I wouldn't have discovered Andrew's sorry secret! I wouldn't have run, and I wouldn't be standing here with Rafe now...*

They drank in companionable silence for a few moments.

"Okay," she said finally her nerves getting the best of her as she wondered if she would be able to pull this off. "What do you want me to fix?"

"We'll be traditional today. Eggs, bacon and toast." He set his empty cup down and turned to the refrigerator and began pulling things out.

"Where are the frying pans and baking pans?"

He pointed to the cabinet. "Griddle and skillet are in there."

She grabbed them and set them on the stove. He set the eggs and bacon on the counter and then pulled a bag of frozen biscuits out of the freezer. Relief rushed over her. She wouldn't be expected to make them from scratch! She might be able to fake breakfast eventually, but not if homemade biscuits were involved. To her surprise and relief, he actually did most of the work. Sadie watched closely, knowing that tomorrow would be her turn. If at all possible, she wanted to do a good job and not embarrass herself completely.

She was very aware of him standing beside her as they worked, and she was fascinated by his efficiency in the kitchen. There were three other amazingly handsome cowboys in the house, but none of them made her heart skip with awareness.

Rafe was glad when the others came in a few

minutes after they started cooking. Sadie had a pair of Maddie's shorts and a pink T-shirt on. Simple, but he was having a terrible time concentrating. She was quiet today, and he was curious about what she was thinking. He wondered how her night had gone, and if there had been more phone calls after she'd gone to her room after the party.

He was curious about everything to do with her. Holding her in his arms during the dance had been sweet torture to him, as he'd had to keep fighting off the urge to pull her close and have her lay her head on his shoulder as their bodies moved together to the music. He'd decided soon after the second dance that dancing wasn't a good idea because his good sense kept ebbing and he'd been in serious trouble trying not to lose his head.

But he behaved himself and hoped that after they got to know each other better that she might confide in him.

Rafe realized as they were cooking that she had been more than honest where cooking was concerned. The woman didn't know much at all. But he didn't care and carefully tried to make it easier on her. Hopefully she would be able to learn quickly.

Of course that was one more question he had

about her. What woman didn't know a little about cooking?

Maybe that was a chauvinistic thought on his part, but almost every woman he'd ever known knew something. He'd come to the conclusion as he showed Sadie how to scramble eggs that she might not even know how to boil an egg, much less fry or scramble one.

He still didn't care and decided he'd come down and help her cook every morning if she were standing beside him with her arm brushing his while she sprinkled pepper on the eggs.

Yup, he had it bad…

"Morning, ma'am," Chase said, coming in from outside and tipping his hat at Sadie before hanging it on the long hat rack next to the door. "It sure smells appealing in here."

Ty and Dalton came in right behind him.

"Thanks, but Rafe did most of it this morning," Sadie admitted, smiling so appealingly that Rafe knew good and well that as long as she smiled at them like that, his partners wouldn't complain. "I've just never cooked before. Growing up, we had a cook, and she took her domain seriously. But I'm a fast learner." Sadie laughed.

So that was one question answered, Rafe noted,

as they all sat down at the table and filled their plates and grinned at her like fools. Did he look that dopey?

"These are great eggs," Chase said immediately. He obviously had gone deaf.

Sadie waved a hand. "Remember, not me but Rafe."

"Well, it probably tastes so good because of your pretty presence in the room," Chase added without missing a beat, and then winked at her. "His eggs never tasted this good before."

Heat crawled up Rafe's neck as he began to feel territorial. He shot Chase a tight warning. Chase kept right on grinning at Sadie.

She looked a little perplexed as chuckles rolled around the room as all his partners shot looks at him. They were yanking his chain, he realized, and that made him all the more hot.

"So, you joining us to work cattle today?" Dalton asked, barely hiding the fact that he saw the back-off warnings Rafe was sending out. He was clearly giving Rafe a hard time.

All of his partners knew that Rafe hadn't dated much in the last few years. They also knew that, given his personality, his sudden interest in Sadie was an uncommon affair. So of course he was going to have to endure a steady razzing during the day to come. So be it.

Sadie missed the interaction between him and Chase as she looked up from her plate with startled eyes. "Me? Work cows? Oh no, no, no, not happening. The kitchen is going to be a learning experience enough."

Ty paused, lifting his cup to his mouth. His lip twitched as if he was fighting not to smile. "We're going to be out there without time to stop. Do you think you could scrounge up some sandwiches and fixin's and bring them out to us in one of the trucks?"

"That would be a great idea," Dalton added, grinning openly. "What do y'all think about Ty's idea?"

Chase nodded. "Ranks right up there with Rafe hiring Sadie on as cook. Great thinking."

Liking the idea of seeing Sadie at noon, Rafe joined in with a smile. "I like it. I'll give you instructions on where to come."

Sadie looked a little overwhelmed. "Sure. You're all paying me, so I'll try to do what you'd like."

"Don't look so worried," Rafe said. "No chuck wagon meal or anything. Just some simple sandwiches is all."

Truth was that Rafe didn't care if she brought food or not, as long as she showed up and he got to see her smiling face in another few hours.

Chase stood. "We better head that way, boys. Daylight's burning. Thanks for breakfast. We'll see you in a bit." He winked again, and Rafe thought about giving him a boot in the backside. "This ranch just got even more appealing since you came along." With that, he snagged his hat and strode out the door. *Sauntered* was more like it.

Rafe felt that territorial heat rolling through him again. Chase Hartley had a way with the women, and he knew it and used it. He was trying to rile him.

As the others said goodbye and headed off, Rafe strode to the corner of the kitchen, grabbed a pen and note pad from a drawer, and quickly drew a map.

Sadie came over to him. "Thanks. I'll clean up. That I know how to do. So sandwiches are really fine to fix?"

"Yup. The fridge is full of stuff to fix them, and the pantry has a bunch of bags of chips." He slid the instructions over to her, but studied her. "Are you sure you're okay today? I didn't want to leave without asking. Since I know you had something rough going on yesterday."

She took a deep breath. "I'm fine. I'm just dealing with some issues. I think time is going to help."

"You know, I'm a good listener. I promise. Sometimes just telling someone else your problems can ease the strain." He gave her an encouraging smile. "I've gotten through my own share of troubles over the years, just so you know."

She stared out the kitchen window for a moment. Then looked at him with stormy eyes. He wanted in that instant to fold her into his arms and hold her. "You can trust me, Sadie," he urged, feeling compelled to push a bit.

Her expression faltered. "I-I was supposed to get married in a week," she rattled out after a moment of hesitation. "I ran off yesterday."

There were a lot of things she could have said, but that was not what he'd been expecting. *"Married."*

She nodded. "Yeah, you heard right. Married." She took a deep breath. "I found my fiancé in, let's just say, a compromising position yesterday, and I ran. Just got in my car and drove."

"So you are technically a runaway bride?"

She nodded. "I ran. I didn't call it off. I just got

in my car and drove and didn't tell anyone until I talked to my mother last night right after we got our food. I just drove for four hours and didn't stop until I had that flat. My mother was at the engagement party wondering where I was when I returned her call last night." She grimaced. "Terrible, isn't it? *I'm* terrible."

He had to grimace. "Yeah, probably not the easiest way for her to find out there wasn't going to be a wedding. But you had to be in shock yourself."

"I'm not proud at all, but you're right. I wasn't exactly thinking straight."

"I'm sorry you had to find that out about your fiancé. But I'm glad you found it out before the wedding."

"Me too," she said, sighing. "I knew things weren't right between us though. That's why I had dropped by his apartment. To talk to him. To maybe break it off."

"I see. So you were already having cold feet." Rafe hadn't missed the "maybe." He wondered why she'd known things weren't right and wondered if that was because her heart wasn't feeling it or if her heart was broken because she'd just sensed her fiancé wasn't behaving right. The distinction was important to him, he realized.

"I have to ask, though you've explained some. I'm still confused about the bunny suit."

"Well, I went for my weekly visit to the pediatric wing at several of the hospitals around Houston. I had been at M. D. Anderson Cancer Center downtown, and I stopped by to talk to Andrew…" She paused, her brow knitted, and then her eyes flared wide. "I found him entertaining his, um, girlfriend. I was wearing my *bunny suit*. I mean, really, think about that. Talk about bizarre. I mean, I was standing there in my floppy feet and big belly and--"

She inhaled while Rafe went cold inside. Poor Sadie.

Her voice faltered. "It was just a hard position to find myself in. I just fled. I drove for four hours. I guess if I hadn't had the flat tire, I'd have driven to Alaska or something. But I had it, and then you stopped and helped me, and here I am."

Rafe couldn't help himself. He reached for Sadie, wrapped his arms around her and pulled her close. She came easily, and her warmth seeped into him. He just wanted to help her past the overwhelming hurt he could read in her eyes, though he sensed she was trying hard to hide it.

"I'm so sorry that happened to you." He

stroked her hair, all the while wanting to take the guy who'd hurt her and break him into pieces. How could he do that? Rafe knew that emotion she was feeling. He'd lived it. When he'd been at his lowest, he'd experienced almost the same devastating blow with his fiancée.

"You'll get through this," he murmured, loving the way she laid her head against his shoulder as she just let him hold her. The faint sweet scent of her hair drew him closer, and he had to remind himself he was consoling her, not holding her for his own agenda. Which was because he was drawn to her more than he'd ever been drawn to anyone, even Dawn.

Swift, sudden heat rushed through him. She lifted her face to his, and every cell in his body tensed. She was gorgeous, and those gigantic green eyes sucked him in. He focused. She surprised him more when she pulled away, backing out of his arms. A heated blush colored her cheeks.

"I will get through this, and part of it will be because you helped me fix my tire and gave me this job. And you've been so very kind. Thank you. Now, I need to get this kitchen cleaned up and then get started on lunch," she said fussily, as if she were needing the busyness to keep from saying more. Or maybe feeling more. Rafe liked that she was putting on a determined, brave face. It made him admire her.

"If you need to talk, let me know. No strings attached, I promise."

"Thank you. Being busy will help me get through this."

He nodded. "Whatever it takes. Keys are in the truck. The white one parked by the stables. Those instructions will get you out to the pasture." He tipped his hat, then spun on his boot and headed toward the back door. "I've got to go, but call if you need anything. All of our numbers are on a pad by the phone." He strode to the door, then looked back at her.

She smiled. "Thanks," she said, her voice huskier than it had been, making him wonder if she was about to cry. Or was she feeling what he was feeling?

No, she'd just lived through a hard time, so she was about to cry. That was more logical. Because one thing he knew, what he was feeling for this near stranger was illogical.

Completely illogical. With one last look over his shoulder, he nodded at her, then fled into the morning. Any longer, and he'd have strode back across the kitchen and snatched her to him and planted a kiss so full of longing on her tempting lips that he'd have scared her off and sent her on the run again.

When he reached his truck he looked back to see Sadie standing in the doorway watching him leave. He felt like a spooked mustang heading for high ground. She lifted a hand in farewell, and something in the pit of his stomach warmed. Again, he had to fight the overwhelming urge to stalk back to that porch and kiss her senseless.

The warmth curled tighter. He paused, drank her in like he was dying of thirst, then forced himself to point his truck toward the exit and head out.

He might not have wanted to admit it earlier, but there was no doubt that Sadie affected him more than any woman had in a very long time.

The question was, what was he going to do about it?

CHAPTER SEVEN

Feeling blindsided by the way Rafe affected her, Sadie watched him drive off. Then she hurried inside and started rummaging through the fridge. She had hours before she needed to deliver lunch to the designated spot, but she wanted to make certain everything was in order. Plus she needed to keep busy.

Her phone started vibrating at about eight o'clock.

Her mother.

Then Andrew texted. "Call me. This is ridiculous, Sadie. You're embarrassing me AND your parents. Get back here. What you think you witnessed was not what you think."

Sadie's blood pressure shot up. *Oh really? Then what exactly was it?* Adriana had been engulfed by his arms, and they were kissing as if there was no tomorrow. It had not been a kiss one could *mis*interpret.

Seething, Sadie read the rest of the text: "Sadie, I love you. We have a beautiful wedding planned. Guests are still coming, and the fact that you missed the engagement party has people talking."

What? He hadn't called off the wedding?

Sadie dialed her mother.

Evelyn picked up on the first ring. "Have you come to your senses?"

"I have all my faculties, Mother. Please tell me that you called the wedding off."

"No. Andrew said you were just having cold feet. He is heartbroken. You should see him. He was a shell of a man without you. I told him you told me to cancel the wedding, but he said he just couldn't do it that. He would prove to you that he loves you and that you'll be home this week and the wedding will go on as planned."

"Mother--" Was Sadie even speaking to the woman who'd raised her? "I know that you had your heart set on this wedding and that you have poured your every breath into the preparations, and I am so sorry that this has happened. But I don't love Andrew. I cared about him, about the man I thought he was, the man who had his sights set on

75

helping get things done through running for office and heading to Washington. But he's not the man I thought he was."

"He's a good man. You'll have a good life with him. You'll move in the right circles--"

"I don't love him. I know that now, and I'm so sorry to put you through this embarrassment. But I'm making the calls myself and putting an end to this."

Her thoughts were running rampant. When her friends had been texting to see how she was doing, they were thinking she was sick, not that she'd called off the wedding. Sadie groaned. A pin drop could have been heard because of the silence on the other end of the line. Sadie felt for her mother. Yes, her mother had pressured her that she needed to find a husband. That there were certain qualities in a man that were expected. A lawyer with a political agenda was high on that expectation list. Mom had even introduced Sadie to Andrew.

But, Sadie knew that ultimately this fiasco was her fault. And it was up to her to make the calls, and if she had to, she would go back to Houston and deal with this once and for all.

No more running.

Rafe was surprised to see Sadie driving across the pasture at eleven. She'd come early. He took his hat off and swiped his shirt sleeve across his forehead, then urged his horse to head her way.

"You found us," he said, smiling down at her through the open window.

"You drew me a very good map to follow," she said. "Where should I park and set up. I'm early. I hope that's okay."

"Sure. We've been wrestling with calves all morning, so we don't mind breaking early."

"I was thinking I could set it up, and if this was too early, y'all could eat when you wanted to."

"Nope. Like I said, it's fine. You can park the truck under that oak tree over there." He nodded toward a huge old oak that stood in the center of the pasture.

She headed that way and he followed on his horse. She had on a pair of jeans that Maddie must have left her and a bright red T-shirt, simple and nothing special, but seeing her just brightened his day. He swung out of the saddle and met her at the tailgate of the truck.

"We could get used to this," he said.

She stopped and looked earnestly at him. "It

77

seems like a good idea. Rafe, I need to tell you something. Or ask you something, I guess," she said, in a rush.

"Sure. I'm listening."

"I spoke to my mother. And I was really hit by what I'd done." She paused, heaving in a deep breath.

Rafe jerked, feeling as if he'd just gotten a fist to the gut. Was she sorry she'd called off her wedding? His mother had repeatedly put up with emotional and physical abuse from his father. In his mind, if Sadie went through with her wedding, she was doomed to live a life of repeated emotional abuse. He didn't want that for her. Couldn't stand the thought of it.

"You had a good reason for needing some space."

She didn't look convinced. "Maybe, but my mother shouldn't have to deal with this alone."

"Maybe so, but I don't see any reason why you can't give yourself a few days to get your head on straight." He wasn't going to tell her she needed to go back and face the music, because he believed she'd needed to run from a bad situation.

"I'm ashamed that I ran. I'm not even sure why I did it. I should have taken care of it all and stayed.

I left it for my mother to handle, and that was completely unfair to her. Andrew is telling everyone that I was sick last night, but that everything is fine. My mother believes I should marry him. It's a mess."

"It sounds like it. Certainly doesn't sound like the happy experience getting married is supposed to be." Rafe was proud that she realized running from her problems might not have been the right way to handle calling off the wedding. But he wasn't unhappy at all about meeting her. And if her running was the reason they'd met, then he wasn't going to wish she'd done something differently.

He wasn't ready for her to leave. "Do you think there is a chance that you'll reconsider marrying this jerk?" He called it like he saw it, and he could be calling the sleaze of a man far worse than jerk or sleaze.

"No. Yesterday I went to Andrew's apartment to call off the wedding. Now, after what I saw, there isn't anything he could say that would convince me."

Rafe knew it wasn't any of his business. But maybe it was because of his background of watching his mother cave again and again that he just couldn't be comfortable believing she was telling the truth. That worried him, but he didn't say that aloud.

"I'm glad," he said instead. "You deserve better, Sadie." He held her troubled eyes and had to fight off reaching for her again. *t was a growing need in him, this desire to hold her close. To protect her. But he barely knew her. "The job is yours for as long as you want it."

A smile curled sweetly at the corners of her mouth. "Thanks. That being so, I guess I'd better get busy."

He grinned and told himself to pull back. "Do you need help?"

She stuffed her fist to her hips. "Rafe, you're my boss. I might have needed you for breakfast, but I've got the sandwich department under control. Believe me, I know three things when it comes to food: sandwiches, microwaveable food and takeout."

He laughed at that, shook his head and then headed to his horse. "I'll go tag a few more calves, then bring the others back with me in about fifteen minutes. How's that?"

She'd turned to pull the tailgate down and now looked over her shoulder at him. "That sounds perfect."

He groaned inwardly and climbed into the saddle and rode back to the others. But all he could think about was that she might leave before the week was over.

Sadie watched the men of New Horizon Ranch riding toward her. The men and Maddie. Sadie was still curious about this partnership and how it worked. But for now, as the partners and the other cowboys who worked the ranch rode her way, she was amazed that she was here. If she'd asked any of her friends two days ago if they saw her on a ranch, they'd have laughed. But here she was, and she could not help smiling at the picture they made riding toward her. Her gaze was drawn to Rafe, and goosebumps prickled across her skin as she watch him lead the group. He sat straight but relaxed in the saddle as he loped toward her. The man looked like he was leading a posse across the ranch, and with the way his gaze was pinned on her, Sadie felt like she was his target. The thought lifted her spirits as warmth filled her. She'd let him take her into custody any time.

The man was oh-so-fine, and she realized--as her heart raced out of control--that she was in oh-so-much trouble. This out of control attraction so soon after calling off her wedding was terrifying. Rebound maybe?

She needed to pull back on the crazy feelings and start putting some distance between the too-soon-to-be-taken-seriously emotions overtaking her. And she needed to do it right now.

Sadie just wasn't at all sure that she wanted to.

And that was a very dangerous thought.

CHAPTER EIGHT

Sadie was glad Rafe had told her there would be ten people working the cattle, so she'd fixed more than enough sandwiches for everyone to have at least two. The men all moved to a water jug that was sitting in a holder attached to the truck and began one at a time pushing the button and washing their hands with the container of soap hanging off the side. She wasn't sure if it was common to have a hand washing station attached to a truck, but she had to say she liked it.

"Hey, Sadie," Maddie called, making her way over to her. She looked like the working cowgirl that she was. She wore red chaps over her jeans and a red bandana tied around her forehead beneath her straw western hat. Her chaps dragged the ground just enough that her boots peeked out as she walked. Sadie was completely impressed with

Maddie hanging in there working with all these men.

"Hey to you. Good grief. I can't believe you do this," Sadie said, honestly.

Maddie laughed and stuffed her fist on her slim hips. "I love it. I'm not the only female who ever sweated a little and ate dust working cattle with the guys. Who says cowboys get to have all the fun?"

"I wouldn't know the first thing about something like that."

"While you're here, you should saddle up and come work with us one day."

Sadie wasn't so sure that sounded appealing. True, she would probably enjoy watching Rafe work. But getting in there with those cattle herself? "I'll take your word for it."

Maddie just shook her head. "I'm telling you, you're missing out. Of course by the time I get in, I reek of cow, and there is no telling what kind of germs are crawling around on me and these sodbusters."

"Stop being a girl," Chase said, shooting Maddie a teasing glare. His eyes were twinkling, as if he knew he was pushing Maddie's buttons.

She shot him a glare right back. "What can I say. I love my job, but I am a girl."

They continued to tease each other all through the meal. Sadie enjoyed being around the whole group.

"Do you ride?" Rafe asked her when they'd finished eating.

"I've...ridden at the stables some." There was a stable near the exclusive neighborhood where she'd been raised, and her parents had made it a point to have her ride. But she'd never ridden in the open pastures.

"That's good. I need to ride out and check on some strays, so would you like to come along? It'll give you some fresh air and new perspective."

"I need to take the truck back--"

"Maddie was getting ready to head back to meet Cliff. Hey, Maddie, instead of loading up your ride, I think I'm going to take Sadie with me to check the calves. What do you think?"

"That's perfect. Sadie if you're going to be here, you need to see the ranch the way we do. You'll love it. This place is amazing. Do you live in the country or in the city?"

"I live in the city. Not downtown, but my apartment isn't in the country at all. And my mother lives close."

Everyone stopped eating to look at her as if she

were an alien from outer space or something.

Ty hiked up a very nice eyebrow beneath his cowboy hat. "That should be against the law, living surrounded by all that concrete."

She laughed when several grunts of agreement sounded from the cowboys.

"I happen to like living near the mall and civilization." That had everyone halting their chewing to gawk at her.

Maddie nudged her. "These boys would never, ever understand that statement, so don't even try to state your case. Just hop on my horse and see the other side of the coin. You don't have to love it, but I bet you'll like it a lot. At least you'll understand why you're getting the evil eye from these spur-wearing, slow-drawling, handsome hunks of pure male ty-test-ter-rone."

The way she said testosterone caused the evil-eyed cowboys to nearly fall over with laughter and more grunts of approval. Rafe smiled lazily at her, and she was certain he had been having a very good time watching the exchange.

Rafe didn't waste any time in getting Sadie on Maddie's horse so she could ride beside him across the pasture. He wanted to get to know her better, and there was no time like now. He also wanted to know what she was thinking and feeling. If he could help her, then he wanted to do that. And that included finding out more about this supposed ex-fiancé who believed she was going to show up on Saturday night despite what he'd done to her.

Not if Rafe could help it.

"You ride good," he said, watching her move easily with the horse.

"I'm a little stiff."

"You looked nervous too, but that's probably because you needed some time to relax and get used to being in the saddle again. But you've got it."

She shot him an appreciative look between a smile and grimace, and he laughed. "Come on, it's not that bad."

"No, I was just thinking about being sore tomorrow after letting you talk me into this."

"Oh, yeah, you might be right about that if we ride too long. If you enjoy riding, though, there are plenty of horses, so any time you want to, just let me know."

"Thanks. This place really is beautiful, and that pasture there is so green."

DEBRA CLOPTON

They'd ridden across the open pasture and were almost to a stand of oak trees surrounded by a carpet of lush green grass. He dismounted and opened the gate. "We've got oats planted in this area, so we have to keep the cattle out for now. That's what you're seeing that's so green."

"I imagine the cattle can't wait. You know, with the grass truly being greener on the other side of the fence right now."

"So you have a little humor going on inside that pretty head of yours."

She laughed as he closed the gate behind her, then swung back into his saddle. "I wear a bunny costume, remember? I have to have a little personality to pull that off."

"True. So, tell me about that. What got you started wearing that cute little cottontail outfit?"

She tossed her hair over her shoulder, and her eyes twinkled when she looked his way. "I just wanted to make kids smile."

"Yes, but you chose sick kids to make smile."

"Not always. I go to women's shelters and do programs for the children who are there, just like I'm going to do at the shelter here in town. I do a lot of different things."

"I admire you for that. What got you started?"

She looked almost embarrassed as she looked away, and they rode in silence for a moment. "Okay, so, here goes. I was sitting at a stop sign one day and, believe it or not, I glance over at this car on the side of the road that has steam billowing from beneath the hood. It had obviously just pulled over, because in that moment the door opened and a headless bunny stepped out."

"No way."

"Scout's honor. Very similar to the way you found me. She frantically waved me down, and I pulled over, as much out of shock as anything. She was on her way to see a bunch of kids at a pediatric ward, and she was almost in tears worrying that she was going to stand them up since her car was broken down. I told her I'd take her, and I did. She'd been very sick as a kid, had a brain tumor that they'd been able to remove, but she'd spent a lot of time in the pediatric ward. This was her way of giving back."

"Wow. I've never thought of something like that."

"Me either. I went in with her, and it really kind of scared me at first. You know, I was just out of my element. But when I saw the excitement on those little faces and the way they responded to

89

Amber, it just…oh, Rafe, there are just no words to explain what it did to me. It grabbed hold of me, and I knew I wanted to see more of that. Within a month, Amber had me in a suit and helped me start my own volunteer program. I've been doing this for about two months now."

"That's incredible."

"I love it."

"So, what do you do to make a living?"

"I-I live off of a trust."

He caught the embarrassed way she said it. He had to admit that she didn't strike him as the type to live off of Daddy's money fulltime. He wasn't exactly sure how to react to that. It was such a different picture than what he'd assumed. "That must be nice."

She colored a deep burgundy. "Yeah, tell me about it." She stiffened and didn't look at him.

He pulled his horse to a halt. "Whoa, I didn't mean to judge you."

"Why not? Up until that day, I had no real problem drawing my allowance and believing I deserved it just because my granddad had a few oil wells."

"I don't believe that."

"Oh, believe it. It's true. And thus, in part, the

reason I was engaged to Andrew in the first place. He's everything my mother hoped for in a match for me. Ever since my father passed away a few years ago, she's been obsessed with finding me the right kind of husband. And I just went along with it because…"

"Because why?" Rafe didn't know what to think from the information he was getting. If he'd hoped to get to know Sadie better, he'd certainly learned more about her. But know her? -Now he was completely lost on that subject. Sadie wasn't matching up to anything he'd assumed about her. And he wasn't sure he was liking what he was hearing.

They'd reached the other pasture, and Rafe dismounted to open the gate and waited while she walked her horse through. He was silent, and she didn't blame him. Sometimes Sadie looked back on herself and wondered what she had been thinking. It was as if she'd been sleepwalking through her life until Amber had shown her another world. A world that grabbed her by the heart and had made her start questioning everything about herself. Even her engagement.

And now she'd met a man who stirred things deep within her heart and caused her to know that calling off the wedding had been the right thing to do, even if she hadn't caught Andrew with his girlfriend. It was the right thing to do because she didn't love him like she'd dreamed of loving someone one day. She'd simply been settling.

And now she'd met this wonderful cowboy who, as crazy as it seemed, had in the short time since they'd met captured more of her heart than anyone ever had. And now with his quietness, she knew he was wondering how she could have lived her whole life in such a vacuum.

"The calves and cattle we're looking for are going to be in this pasture, since this is where we moved them from last," he said when he was back in the saddle. "At least that's what we hope. If not, then they've somehow gotten into other pastures and will take longer to locate."

"Could they be in among those trees?" she asked, suddenly feeling awkward. He'd asked why, and she'd yet to answer him.

"That's where we're going. We counted earlier, and we're missing one that should have been in the group we were vaccinating."

Sadie followed him into the shadows of the

trees. The sunlight filtered through the thick canopy, giving a hazy aura to the woods that reminded her of the haze in her emotions at the moment as she studied Rafe's solid back. Tangled underbrush lined the area, but the horses kept their feet on the thin trail weaving through the trees.

"What made this trail?" she asked, more for something to fill the awkward silence between them than because she wanted to know.

"The cows. They come in here when they're hot and nosey."

They had ridden fairly deep into the woods, and she could hear the gurgle of water. There must be a stream or river or something further into the woods. Sure enough, within moments they were at the edge of a pretty good sized stream.

"Rafe, a calf. It's stuck in the mud." She headed her horse down the bank. Rafe was behind her, but she hurried toward the animal. It was mired deeply in the mucky water. Sadie scrambled out of her saddle before Rafe caught up to her.

It wasn't too big, but it wasn't tiny either. It was lying on its side with three legs buried in the mud.

"Sadie, stop," Rafe called.

But she was already ankle deep in the mud, determined to help the poor creature.

It had been in the mud long enough that it barely had made a sound as she headed its way. She didn't hesitate as she reached the baby and, despite being knee-deep in the mud, she slugged close to stand behind it, bent forward and tried to lift it.

"Sadie."

She looked at Rafe. His shock at her actions was written on his face. "We need to get him out," she said, ignoring the idea that he probably thought she was crazy.

He didn't hesitate, either, but dismounted and slogged through the mud to stand at the calf's head. "You push, and I'll pull."

Rafe dipped his hands into the mud and grabbed the calf by the front legs. Sadie was already in position, and she pushed. The calf didn't move at first, but it did bawl better than it had since she'd spotted it. Without needing to be told she pushed again. Then, with the two of them working together, the calf came loose from the mud. The only problem was that when it did Sadie had pushed so hard, the calf jerked and propelled forward to safety. Sadie and Rafe weren't so lucky. They both lost their balance and landed in the mud.

They looked at each other and began to chuckle.

"Sadie," he said, lifting a hand out of the mud

to tap her on the nose with muck. "You are full of surprises. Hauling off into the mud was not what I expected."

She sobered, wrinkling her nose, which was now dotted with mud. "The calf needed help, and that's all I thought about."

"Despite the mud."

She pushed up to her knees. "It washes off."

He grinned. "Yes, it does." And then he startled her when he hauled her into his arms and marched straight into the stream with her.

CHAPTER NINE

Rafe had lost his mind. He knew it the moment he'd watched Sadie tromp into that mud after that calf. Yup, all thoughts, coherent or otherwise. Vanished, replaced by the glaring desire for this woman. Not just desire for her, but to have her. He wanted Sadie.

Wanted to kiss her, to hold her, to have her. And not just in a physical way. He wanted her in his life. And he had known her for less than one day! He was not an irrational man. He was serious. Jaded. Cautious.

But right then and there, he didn't care about any of that.

He didn't analyze his feelings. He just scooped Sadie out of mud and into his arms and carried her into the stream and strode right out into the chest deep water with her. He wasn't thinking straight.

Certainly wasn't thinking with the calculated reasoning that he was known for. All he was thinking was about Sadie and this moment.

She gasped at the coolness of the water. Or maybe from his actions. Her arms instinctively wrapped around his neck, and she laughed again, the fullness of it filling him, as if filling every dark, hidden corner of his soul with light. He let her slide to her feet. Then, without another thought, he kissed her.

Water swirled gently around them as his arms tightened protectively around her. When she didn't pull away, he deepened the kiss.

"Sadie," he said, breaking away. "I hope I'm not scaring you, but I've been needing to do that since the first time I saw you."

Her eyes were huge, and he was pretty certain the dazed look he saw in the deep pools of green matched what she was seeing in his dark eyes.

"I know what you mean. But Rafe, I'll be honest and tell you that I'm in a really mixed up time with all I have going on in my life. I-I don't really trust my emotions right now."

He wanted to hug her harder for her honesty. "I understand. It was just a kiss." He picked her up again and walked out of the water with her, heading to a spot down the stream where there was drier land. His boots sloshed water as he strode onto the packed ground and set her on her feet.

It was just a kiss. They stared at each other for a moment, then he strode to where his hat lay and picked it up, all the while struggling to convince himself that, yes, it was just a kiss.

There were a thousand questions he wanted to ask her, needed to ask her. She was a rich kid who'd been engaged to a man with political plans, and a mother--and probably her dad too, before he died, expected nothing less from her than that.

He turned toward her. "We better get back."

"But what about the calf?"

"He's fine. More than likely, he'll be out in the pasture now that he's free. We'll head him toward a pond where he can drink safely, and then I'll come back for him with a trailer and move him. He's a little big to get on the back of a horse and haul back."

She laughed at that. "I was wondering. He's almost too big to call a baby anymore."

"Yeah, believe me, I knew that when he used me as a rug to cross the mud and walk out of that sink hole."

She grinned. "But you were so gallant."

He wanted to kiss her again right then and there. "So, now you know. I'll do anything to impress you."

She tilted her head, eyes sparkling. "I'm impressed, cowboy. Despite the emotional mess my life is right now, despite being soaked to the bone, I'm completely impressed with you. Just so you know."

She strode toward her horse, water dripping from her as she went. He couldn't take his eyes off her and knew whatever this was between them was going to take patience. But there was no way he wasn't planning to find out what exactly it was. He wasn't sure who the first woman was she'd described when she'd talked about herself, but the woman who wore bunny suits to cheer up sick kids and who strode fearlessly into the mud to save a struggling calf did not seem like the kind of woman who liked afternoon tea at the club and hobnobbing with power players. Which was exactly what he pictured when she'd been talking about her parents and this Andrew guy. But that bunny-wearing, mud-diving female who had just kissed him in the stream, *that* woman mesmerized him.

Sadie made it through the next two days with mixed emotions. Rafe had kissed her. She'd kissed him back. And her stomach had been tied in knots ever since. At long last, she called her best friend, Amber, and braced for a well-deserved tongue-lashing.

"Where are you? And why haven't you been taking my calls?" Amber demanded the moment she answered.

Sadie rubbed at the pain between her eyebrows. "Amber, I'm sorry. I've been a little freaked out this week."

"About what? It has something to do with Andrew, doesn't it?" She said Andrew's name like it was a dirty word.

Amber had never been a fan of her fiancé, had never trusted him. Nor did she like the fact that Sadie was settling. She'd been very vocal about it. Had only agreed to be her maid of honor because she'd decided to support Sadie in her march to unhappily-ever-after. Sadie hadn't called her because she wasn't prepared for I-told-you-so.

"Be nice, Amber. And yes, it has something to do with Andrew."

"I knew it!" she erupted. "What did he do? Is the wedding off? Something just didn't feel right at the party when you didn't show up and he told that cockamamie story about you being sick. I went to your house, and you weren't there. I have been about to go berserk since then. Well, if you've gotten my messages, you should have a pretty good idea just how crazed I've been--"

"Amber--".

"It's a good thing you called today, because I was about to go confront the man--"

"Amber, stop. Take a breath. Breathe."

"Okay, okay." She huffed in a breath that could be heard across the phone line. "So, I'm good. Now, *what* is going on?"

"Last Friday after I went to the hospital to visit the kids, I went to Andrew's to tell him that I was having second thoughts and that I wanted to call off the wedding."

"*Yes!* Thank you, Lord. Seriously."

Sadie had to hold the phone away from her ear because of Amber's shouts of joy. "But when I got there, he was engaged in some really heavy kissing with this gorgeous woman."

"I knew he was a *scumbag!* What did you do? Did you hit him?"

"No. I got in my car and started driving. I ended up in Mule Hollow with a flat tire, and this

101

really great cowboy came along and helped me fix it and…and he offered me a job as the cook on his ranch, and I accepted."

"Wait. You're a cook? And you just took off and drove? Andrew didn't say anything about calling off the wedding."

"Yes. Yes. And I know. I just found out from Mother two days ago that he didn't call off the wedding. I thought all the text messages from everyone asking if I was okay and how was I feeling was because the wedding was called off. But they were about me not feeling good."

"I guess I should have clarified. So you're working on a ranch? It sounds fun, except for the cooking part. And what about this cowboy?"

"He's amazing. So handsome and nice and irresistible actually."

"Irresistible?"

Sadie hadn't really meant to say that. But then she'd been talking about Rafe and, after that kiss, "irresistible" was the word that kept coming to her thoughts.

"Sadie, who are you, and where did you put my friend?"

That made Sadie smile. Amber had been thrilled when she'd started doing the bunny ministry, but had asked the same thing then.

"I'm finding my way."

"I am *so* glad. But are you sure you're okay?"

"I'm actually good. Very good. I'm enjoying the three days I've been here. I carried lunch to the field one day and went horseback riding with Rafe to locate a missing calf. We found him stuck in the mud by the river." She paused, then told her friend about the incident, and they both laughed. "And Amber, Rafe kissed me."

"Oh, girl. Really? Wow. How was it?"

"It was wonderful. But I'm so mixed up, and I just can't trust my emotions."

"I think this is great. Who needs to trust their emotions? You need to get the sour wind of Andrew out of your system. This cowboy is perfect. It doesn't have to be permanent. You just stay there, learn to cook and spend time with handsome cowboy. Then come home when you're ready."

"Well, I need to come home and call off the wedding. Mother is in denial and believes I'm coming home to marry Andrew even though I've told her I'm not."

"No, don't come home. Stay there. Don't give the wedding another thought, because I will be happy to take care of this."

"But what are you going to do?"

"Just call off the wedding. And with pleasure. Hey, wait. Mule Hollow. Oh, snap. You are in that town with those matchmaking older ladies. The Matchmakin' Posse of Mule Hollow. I remember now. That place was in the news a lot for a while."

"That's it! That's exactly where I am. Can you believe it?"

"Oh, I'm loving this. Have you met them? The Posse?"

"I have. But just briefly."

"Oh, this is gold. I am in heaven thinking about all of this. I have never been an Andrew fan, so I am thrilled you're calling off the wedding and having this adventure. Just watch out for those women. I hear they are good at what they do, and you need to take it slow. Even with Mr. Irresistible."

Sadie thought about it for a few minutes. "I'll let you know about calling off the wedding for me. It's my responsibility."

"Hey, you forget. I am the maid of honor, and I do believe that cancelling a wedding would fall under my responsibilities. So, if you could find it in your heart to not steal my thunder, I would be ever so grateful."

Sadie laughed. She now felt better about the whole fiasco than she had from the moment she'd gotten in her car and run for the hills. And obviously Amber felt the same relief and joy as she did. "I'll try not to. I'll let you know."

"Soon?"

Sadie laughed shortly. "*Soon*. I feel like I should warn Andrew about this."

"Don't you dare," Amber warned. "Come on. Let me do this for you. You don't owe him anything, not after what he did to you. Stay there. I'll take care of this."

"Okay, fine. Yes, that would actually be a relief."

"*Thank you*. Gotta go. I have business to take care of."

Sadie hung up, then stared at the phone grinning. She didn't have to leave.

And she didn't feel bad about it at all.

"Rafe," Sadie called as she entered the barn, drawing Rafe to look up from brushing down his horse.

"I'm going to run to town and pick up some things. I thought I'd explore the town a little bit, and I'm meeting some of the ladies for morning coffee to discuss me visiting the shelter. But I wanted to double check that you don't need me to do anything for lunch today."

He stared at her standing there in her borrowed clothes, with her hair twisted up in some kind of soft hairdo that had tendrils escaping down her neck and along her jawline. His fingers itched to tug out the clasp and run his fingers through that beautiful, rich copper hair. "No, we're fine. We're going to be working over near the county line, and there's a BBQ place within a mile of that ranch entrance. Thanks. You have a good time. You should have lunch."

"I think I might do that. I also hear there's a really cute boutique there. I might see what they have to offer, since I've decided not to go home on Saturday."

He came to full attention. "You were going home?"

"I thought about it. Briefly. To make sure everything was canceled. But my best friend, aka my maid of honor, is checking on everything."

His heart pounded in his chest. "And you're okay with this?" It had taken every ounce of his will power not to walk into the kitchen the last couple of mornings and take her in his arms and kiss her. It had been harder each evening to say goodnight and then walk out the door. He hadn't gone to his room because he'd known he wouldn't sleep.

"I'm relieved, actually. Does that say terrible things about me? I'm not a complete wimp, but Amber wants to make all the calls. She never liked Andrew. She finally went along with me only because, as she put it, I was going to need all of her support after the deed was done."

He laughed. "That's not exactly funny, but it is. She sounds like someone I'd like."

"Oh, believe me, I'm surprised she didn't tie me up and kidnap me. I just put her aversion to Andrew off as her usual bad-tempered mood where happy-ever-after commitments were concerned."

"She must have had a bad experience."

"She did, but she's never talked about it. So, anyway, I wanted to let you know where I was going and that I'll be hanging around this weekend instead of heading home."

He nodded, thinking and still stunned by the way she affected him. "You have the credit card with you for the groceries, don't you? Please buy lunch on it and anything else you need."

"I have it. But now that my mother knows the

wedding's off, there's no need for me not to access my accounts." She smiled. "I don't know why I thought anyone would be trying to hunt me down through bank info anyway. This is not espionage or anything."

She left soon after that, and he took a deep breath, leaned against the stall and stared at the powerful chestnut horse he'd been brushing down.

"I'm in trouble, Red. But the funny thing is, it doesn't hurt like I thought it would."

He'd had his heart trampled once when he was at his lowest moment and his dreams had been crushed. But as bad as that had been, he was realizing that his heart was resilient.

And, thinking about Sadie, he knew some things were worth risking the pain for.

CHAPTER TEN

Sadie drove to town, her mind locked on thoughts of Rafe. She had to get over this. He'd looked like the sturdy, solid, sexiest cowboy--sexiest man period--that she'd ever seen. And when those deep eyes of his settled on her, it was as if he were touching her, despite the distance between them. Surely he didn't do that to every woman who came around. Falling for a man like him would be an all the time worry for the woman who loved him. A man who looked like he did would have women falling for him all the time. She was being foolish, and she knew it.

She had been around him for a very few days, and already she thought she knew and understood him. Boy, was that tricky. Had she ever thought she knew Andrew? He'd completely deceived her. And she hadn't even been in love with him. Surely she would know when the man she truly loved didn't love her back?

Wouldn't she?

And why was she worrying about that when she was thinking of Rafe? It wasn't as if she'd fallen in love with the man simply because he'd helped her when she needed it, no questions asked. Or that he'd been kind and considerate. Or that, when he kissed her, it was so amazing, it was like a dream? Or that, when she was with him, she felt like no harm could befall her?

Sadie slowed as her thoughts rolled.

How could she feel those things in less than five days? And even if she did feel them, how could she trust something that unbelievable?

She couldn't.

And that was what she told herself sternly. "Your emotions are stressed and can't be trusted right now." Right.

So, she would keep her distance, stay here and work because she wanted to stay away from home a little while longer. And because, despite every argument she could produce, none of them made her able to stop thinking about her cowboy. "Hold on there, Sadie. He is not *your* cowboy. He is just a nice man," she snapped. Thoughts like that were not helping her situation. Being here was helping one problem, but creating a new one that Sadie was beginning to be consumed with.

After the next few miles, town came into view. a sight that was startling because of its color. Why, she was at least five miles away, but it stood out on the horizon, like an Old West clapboard town constructed on the plains out in the middle of nowhere. Its different height buildings were silhouetted against the mid-morning sun except-- she smiled at the sight--every building was painted a bright color. And like a jewel, in the center a very bright, hot pink two-story building beamed out like a calling card. It was so bright and inviting that Sadie pressed the gas pedal and drove a little faster just so she could get there sooner. She loved it. *Loved it!*

And as she drove past the first stores, she wasn't any less in love. Bright window boxes overflowed from second story windows and first floor windows too. And if there wasn't a window box, there was a barrel planter overflowing with flowers that were still thriving from the summer. Red geraniums, pink periwinkles, yellow lantana were the prominent flowers, and they stood out against the vibrant buildings. The mind boggling pink structure was the hair salon, Heavenly Inspirations. The feed store was a bright yellow, the diner bright blue, and there were grass green and rainbow colored buildings. The list went on and on.

Sadie parked her car in front of the salon and got out. Right beside it stood the ladies' clothing store Dottie had told her about. Ashby's Treasures looked like just what Sadie needed.

Before she took two steps, the door of the salon flew open, and women piled out like kids let out of school.

They were all smiles as they came hustling toward her.

Norma Sue planted her hands on her hips. "It is sure nice to see you're still in town. And that you're going to visit at the shelter."

"We sure are pleased to see you. I'm so glad you've stuck around." Esther Mae winked at her. "How's that Rafe doing? He was so sweet to fix your flat."

"He's fine," Sadie said, seeing Adela smile and shake her head as if she wasn't sure what to think of her friend. That made Sadie smile, because she could only imagine that Esther Mae was probably good at shocking her on a regular basis.

Adela laid her delicate hand on her arm. "We're heading over to the diner now. I'm sure Dottie will be along any moment. And Lacy and Sheri are joining us soon also."

"I'd love that."

"Great," Norma Sue said.

Esther Mae opened the door to the salon. "She's coming with us, so we'll see y'all as soon as you get Thelma out from under that dryer and let her get on home to shock ole Bart right out of his John Deere with that new hairdo you just gave her."

Sadie chuckled at Esther Mae's boisterous statement. She could see Lacy through the window waving at her. She waved back.

Adela explained, "Lacy and Sheri are going to meet us. They just have a client to finish up."

They chattered all the way across the street to the diner. Two older men came striding outside as they were approaching. One was tall and thin, with a lean, lined face and bushy brows above alert eyes. The other wasn't short, but he was shorter than the tall man, and he had a kind, plump face and was balding.

"Hey thar," the tall one bellowed as they were standing on the plank sidewalk across the street

113

from him. "Are you the new gal in town? The one they said came to town dressed like Peter Cottontail?"

"Applegate," harrumphed Esther Mae. "We did not say she was dressed like Peter Cottontail."

"It was Flossy," the other man said just as loudly as his friend. He grinned broadly. "You're causing quite a stir, we hear."

Sadie looked curiously from one to the other. "I am?"

"Every new single lady in town causes a stir with these three," the tall one they'd called Applegate boomed, face drooped into a deep frown. "You'd better be ready, because they're liable to have you hitched in a week, if you're not careful."

Sadie held up her hands in front of her. "I don't think so."

Both men got the most comical expressions of pity on their faces.

"Most times, that don't matter one iota with the Posse," the shorter man grunted, scratching his balding head.

"Yup, Stanley is right about that," agreed Applegate. "But then it happens, and they all seem happy. 'cept for a few who hightail it out of here

114

and don't look back."

Sadie's eyes widened, and she tried to keep her alarm from showing.

It must not have worked, because Norma Sue took one look at her and frowned.

"Y'all are scaring her," she said. "Men. They don't know anything."

Sadie realized that the ladies hadn't denied the accusation that they were going to fix her up.

"Okay, hold on." She looked at everyone in the circle. "Maybe I should let y'all know I'm here in town because I just ran off from my wedding. So even thinking of fixing me up would be a waste of time."

Everyone's mouths fell open.

"Get out of here," Esther Mae said shrilly in disbelief. "You're a runaway bride?"

"Well, isn't that something. You'd be our second one of them," Norma Sue offered. "App's granddaughter would be the first. Haley Bell Thornton. Now Haley Bell Sutton and new momma of the cutest little curly headed angel you ever saw."

Applegate nodded. "I have to admit that my Haley come runnin' back here lookin' like a whupped puppy, and they fixed her up and put a smile back on her face. And now I'm a great grandpa, and I could jest shout it out."

"You are shouting," Norma Sue drawled.

Sadie would have smiled at his toothy grin, but the alarm bells were now clanging like a house was on fire.

Norma Sue cocked her head at him. "If you don't put your hearing aid in, you're going to scare that tiny baby into a conniption if you shout at her the way you're shouting at us. You too, Stanley."

"Yup, we know. We're goin' ta get them right now. Haley Bell's cooking lunch fer us."

Stanley poked a thumb in his chest. "I'm getting called her great uncle. How's them apples?" His eyes sparkled. "We better git. You hang in there, young woman. This is a good place to lick your wounds."

Sadie started to deny that she had wounds to lick, but knew that wasn't true. She did. As much as she hated it, she was feeling vulnerable. Andrew had cheated on her for a reason. And though there might be the reasonable excuse that he was just a jerk, there was a part of her that was wounded. Part of her wondered if she'd been lacking in some way.

"Please give Haley our love and that sweet newborn," Adela said.

The men tromped off down the old fashioned boardwalk to their trucks, and Sadie followed the women into the diner.

"This is a great place to meet all the locals," Esther Mae confided as they found a couple of tables and scooted them together. "Of course App and Stanley are in here in the mornings playing checkers and being nosey. But Sam does make a wonderful breakfast."

"And the coffee cake is delicious," Adela added. "My husband's coffee is pretty strong though, so be warned." She winked.

Sam came toward them smiling from ear to ear at her. He was a weathered man, skin as tough as leather, but the kind, warm eyes fit perfectly with the welcoming smile. She'd met him briefly at the engagement party, but he'd been buzzing around like a worker bee making sure everything was perfect for Cliff and Maddie.

"Hello, little lady," he said. "You sure are running with a suspicious crowd."

"You don't say." She looked at the ladies with mock skepticism. "You think I should rethink my situation?" She was starting to suspect she just might need to.

"I shor would." His wrinkled expression turned

solemn in an instant. With an expression like that, the man could probably play a mean hand of poker.

"Sam Green, don't you start scaring this poor girl." Norma Sue popped him lightly on the arm.

About that time the diner doors opened, and Dottie, Lacy and her business partner, Sheri, came hustling in. Lacy's pale silken hair was a mass of hand tossed waves, and it bounced above her shoulders. "We made it!" she said, smiling enthusiastically. "Thelma is looking like a knock out and happily on her way home to stun her hubby. So how are you?" She was hugely pregnant and beaming at Sadie with bright blue eyes. There was just something about her that was happily contagious.

"I'm doing great," Sadie said, and suddenly realized that she was. She might be a little wary of the Posse, but otherwise she couldn't have been better.

Sheri had glossy brown hair that she wore short with a few spiked up places. Both she and Lacy wore jeans paired with colorful, artsy tops. Like her friend, she was pregnant. She gave Sadie a somewhat cocky grin. "Have the ladies married you off yet?"

"Sheri," Dottie laughed. "You are so mean."

"I am not. I'm honest. And the way I see it, she should know up front that these three ladies can't help themselves. They probably already have her future staked out for her."

"She might be right." Sam leaned in, chuckled, then headed back toward the kitchen.

"Oh, hogwash," Esther Mae scolded, laughter crinkling the edges of her eyes. "Y'all stop teasing, and let's sit down and talk about Sadie and her bunny suit going to see the kiddos at No Place Like Home."

They started pulling out chairs, and everyone sank into them.

"I'm glad y'all chose a table," Sheri said, patting her tummy. "There is no way either one of us--" she waved her thumb between herself and Lacy, "-- is gettin' in a booth in our conditions."

"So true," Lacy said, patting her tummy. "Sam, where's App and Stanley? And everyone else? This place is dead this morning."

Sam had come over carrying a coffee pot and five white mugs on each finger of his other hand and a teacup dangled from his other pinky. "They went to see the baby."

"Oh, sweet!" she exclaimed. "It's so cool that we're about to have a herd of babies running around here."

Sheri hiked a brow at Sadie. "It's the water you know," Sheri drawled dryly. "Drink bottled water. And stay away from these three, or you'll end up married and starting a family before lunch is over. Especially since they already have you in their sights. You know you do," she said, meeting Esther Mae's green-eyed glare.

"This is starting to get awkward." Sadie chuckled, but she really had begun to need some air.

"Contrary to what Sheri is telling you, we don't just chunk two people together for the idea of it." Norma Sue pushed back her white Stetson, causing her short, kinky gray hair to bush out about her face. "We don't fix just *anyone* up. They have to be right."

"Absolutely," Esther Mae added, sounding insulted. "There is an art to what we 'Posse' girls do." She made quotation marks in the air when she said "Posse." "And that starts with good ole chemistry. Special chemistry, though. Sheri had several cowboys on a string, but *we* didn't start pushing until Pace came to town."

Sheri gave a teasing smirk. "Y'all just didn't know what to do with me. That's why."

"You know it wasn't that," Norma Sue jumped in. "We saw sparks the minute you two got around each other."

Sadie listened to the entertaining stories and felt uplifted at the easy relationship these women all had together. There was an age difference, with she, Lacy and Sheri being in their late twenties to early thirties, and Dottie maybe a little bit older. The Posse was maybe in their late sixties, but acted like they were a decade younger with their spunky talking. Sadie thought about chemistry and Andrew. They'd had a decent relationship, but her heart hadn't skipped beats when he walked into the room. At least not after the first little while of the relationship. He was handsome. No denying that. And he had an air of confidence about him that she was attracted to. Still, she'd known she was settling just so she could start the family she was longing for. She looked at Sheri and Lacy and their rounded stomachs, and her heart ached at the thought that it would be years before she would get to experience the joy of a child growing within her and the blessing of holding her babies in her arms. It was depressing.

Andrew had been everything her mother wanted and the vehicle for her to get everything she

DEBRA CLOPTON

wanted. That sounded terrible, but it was the honest truth. There hadn't really been great sparks or remarkable chemistry. Those two words instantly brought Rafe to mind. She'd known him a short time and told herself that the way she felt when thinking of him or when he walked into the room was merely because knowing him was new. That it would fade.

"So, you really walked out on your wedding?" Esther Mae asked, pulling Sadie back into the conversation.

Sheri, Lacy and Dottie stared at her in dismay.

"When?" Lacy asked.

"You go, girl," Sheri grunted. "If you had second thoughts, then hit the road is what I say. Run for the hills."

Sadie had to smile at that. "Or Mule Hollow."

"True." Dottie looked genuinely concerned for her. "Are you all right?"

"How you doin' with that?" Norma Sue asked, and everyone seemed to lean in toward Sadie. Adela gave her one of her pats on the arm.

"It's okay. I actually left a week early. The wedding is set for Saturday night." She told them that she'd found him hugging and kissing on someone other than her the day she'd stopped by

122

to call off the wedding. That brought exclamations and more encouragement from the ladies. "I had been at the hospital doing my rounds in my bunny suit and happened to still have it on when I went to see him. Not thinking on my part. I mean, how many women wear a huge, hairy bunny suit to call off an engagement? He and Miss Hot Lips probably got a good laugh over that. And well-deserved. But the weirder thing is that he didn't call the wedding off. Me, I just got in my car and started driving and ended up here."

"It was meant to be." Esther Mae beamed, green eyes sparkling with all kinds of excitement.

"But wait," Sheri said suspiciously. "If the dude didn't call off the wedding, that means he expects you to come running back on Saturday and do the deed?"

"My mother does too."

"Sheesh," Sheri growled. "You're not, though. Right?"

"No. My maid of honor is canceling everything today actually. If he shows up at the church, it will be by himself."

"And you're staying here?" Norma Sue asked. "At the ranch. Around Rafe?"

She nodded. "Rafe has been wonderful to me.

DEBRA CLOPTON

He recognized I was in trouble in more ways than my flat tire when he stopped to help the other day."

Esther Mae grinned. "That's Rafe. He's responsible and seems to be a deep thinker. And I'd think that would make him very considerate."

She smiled. Oh, he was considerate. So much so. "I don't know what I would have done if he hadn't showed up. I guess I'd have done something. But this has been such an adventure so far that it's helping me to cope so much better than I was. I think I was in shock on Saturday when I showed up here."

She realized everyone was studying her and that the Posse had very odd glints in their eyes. "This is a wonderful place," she said. "Y'all have made me feel so welcome."

"We try to accommodate." Norma Sue chuckled. "Ain't that right, y'all?"

"So true," Adela added, along with everyone else. "You just keep doing what you're doing. God has a way of bringing his plans for each of us together--in the most unexpected ways sometimes."

"So, about this hospital visiting," Lacy said. "Do you have an act? What exactly do you do when dressed up? What is your plan for the women's shelter?"

124

Sadie felt relieved to have the subject changed. She began to tell them about what she did when wearing her "Flossy suit," as Rafe called it.

Rafe. She thought about all that speculation in the Posse's eyes and realized that she didn't really mind it at all where he was concerned.

CHAPTER ELEVEN

Something smelled good. Rafe stalked into the kitchen driven to see Sadie today. He closed the door and stopped short. The kitchen was a wreck.

The stove was covered with pots. Pans littered the counters, flour was dusted over portions of the counters, and what looked like tomato sauce dripped over the edge of one of the pots. Sadie stood near the sink and spun the moment he entered. Her eyes were huge with surprise; her rose colored cheeks were dusty white from the flour as was as the red apron she wore.

"Whoa. Did an explosion happen in here?" Just looking at her made him smile. She was beautiful and so out of her element right now.

"You're early!" she exclaimed, glancing around, then looking sheepish. "I wasn't expecting you."

"Clearly," he managed to say while keeping a

somewhat straight face. "So, what exploded?"

She touched her moist forehead with the back of her arm, obviously having had her face over the heated oven for a long time. "Nothing. Not so far anyway. But it's a miracle," she said, then beamed. "I made a lasagna. A homemade lasagna. I know it's a wreck, but I think it's going to be great. Esther Mae Wilcox swears by it. She says it's no fail and far superior to the one I was going to buy at the store."

He strode to her then, unable to keep his distance. He gently moved a strand of hair from where it had stuck to her damp cheek. "If you cooked it, I'm all in. This is amazing. You look like you're enjoying yourself."

"I am. I never really took the time to bake or cook, but with nothing else to do and also knowing this is my job, I've been surprised at how much I do love it. But I want to do a good job." She was rattling the words out at a rapid clip, breathless, as if she'd run a mile. He fought a smile because, judging by the mess all around them, it looked like she'd cooked for an army.

He loved her.

Yeah, it was crazy, and he knew it.

He'd known her a week, but he'd basically been

hooked the moment she'd rolled over in her ridiculous hairy suit, and he'd first looked into those green eyes. It was the craziest thing. He'd never believed it would happen to him. It sounded like the first thing Cliff had said about Maddie. Literally.

Sure, it might not be love at first sight, but if it wasn't, it sure felt like it. He hadn't been able to think about anything from the moment he'd seen her on the side of the road. Sure, it had happened to Cliff, but though they were twins, he'd never believed they'd share something like this. Cliff had fallen in love with Maddie at first sight, but Rafe hadn't believed it at first. Hadn't believed something like that was possible. Yet Cliff had told him when it happened, it happened. And that was true.

Rafe had been through a lot in his life. A past he didn't think about often, didn't let himself think about because there was no changing it. He'd had a no-good father who beat his mom when he and Cliff were growing up and a mother who'd refused to leave him. It had been a bad and regretful childhood, and when they were barely seventeen, his mother had gotten ill and died. His dad had stopped raising his hand to their mom after they'd gotten old enough to warn him off, but no amount of begging had gotten her to leave the man. With her dead, he and Cliff had nothing to stay for and had left home and never looked back.

They'd both had dreams of rodeo fame, Cliff on bulls and Rafe in calf roping. He'd also had dreams of falling in love and having a happy future. A misplaced foot on a dismount had ended his rodeo future, and that had ended his engagement. The only thing that had saved him from falling apart was winding up here on New Horizon Ranch with a boss who believed in him and showed him that there was contentment and happiness apart from dashed dreams. But until now, until Sadie had walked into his life, he'd never known completely what a future could look like.

Looking at her now, rumpled, flushed and as sexy as all get out with flour on her cheeks and Italian sauce on her apron, Rafe saw exactly what he wanted. She stood very still as he brushed the flour from one cheek with the pad of his thumb. Then, with all the will power he possessed, he dropped a very restrained kiss to her lips, testing the waters to her feelings. Would she push him away? She'd said she wasn't ready for what was happening between them that day at the stream, but he couldn't help pushing her resolve.

Not when he knew that if he had his way, he'd go down on one knee right there in the kitchen and ask her to marry him.

She wasn't ready though.

If he said anything, she'd run like, well, like a rabbit.

She stepped back, held up a hand between them. "Hold on. Stay right there."

He grinned. "Okay. But it's sure hard to do with you looking so beautiful right now."

She laughed shakily. "Right. I'm a terrible mess."

He shook his head, looking down her. "Nope. Not at all. You're perfect. And you look plum edible actually." He arched a brow, and her eyes dropped to his lips. He smiled his best smile, wanting with everything he had for her to want him as much as he wanted her.

She took a breath as she seemed to sway slightly his way.

He dipped his head, intent on getting that kiss, tasting her tempting lips. Not touching her with anything but his lips, he brushed his over hers, felt her rise on her toes to meet him. And everything in his life seemed to click into place.

Sadie sank into Rafe, mesmerized by his words. The look of desire in his eyes blindsided her. Holy-maca-doo, the man knocked the breath right out of her.

Her hands wound around his neck. She wanted his lips on hers again, wanted his arms wound tightly around her. Wanted his lips, warm, firm and fantastic as they claimed hers. Fire sizzled through her. She stepped closer, meeting him. Bells started ringing! It was like nothing she'd ever experienced. Bells, alarms. Her pulse quickened, her heart leapt--

"There's a buzzer going off," Rafe murmured against her lips.

Dazed and confused, Sadie tried to comprehend his words. "Buzzer?" she murmured, drowning in the feel of him. "Buzzers!" She jerked away. Spun. "The lasagna!"

The buzzer was sounding the alarm. But it sounded nothing like the ones exploding in her head from Rafe's kiss. She snapped the button off and fumbled for the hot pads.

Rafe chuckled behind her, and that didn't help the way her hands shook as she clutched the hot pads. The man did something to her mind, her heart. The man made her crazy.

In a wonderful way.

A very unbelievable, undeniable way.

She pulled open the oven door, and heat flashed over her as she carefully reached for the cookie sheet. This was her first ever lasagna, and she was really excited and horribly nervous about it. She tried not to think about the hot cowboy behind her and concentrated on the hot dish in front of her.

Goodness, it felt heavier than it had when she put it in. A lasagna to feed all these men was huge. When she'd just about gotten out, the cookie sheet slid from the wire rack and suddenly dipped. The large metal pan Esther Mae had suggested she bake it in slid toward the edge. "Oh no!" she exclaimed horrified at what she was seeing. She tried to straighten the edgeless cookie sheet, but that didn't save the casserole on its kamikaze slide instead. Her jerking the cookie sheet caused the lasagna to flip--

"It's go-go-go-ing!"

"Whoa!" Rafe yelped as they both watched it flip over and land upside down on the crack between the door and the oven. Sadie and Rafe looked at each other in disbelief. The only sound in the room was a very odd slurping sound that drew both of them to stare back at the pan.

"My lasagna," Sadie squeaked.

Rafe grabbed the hot pad and lifted the pan, hoping maybe some of it was still inside and could be salvaged. Sadie looked so stricken. But the pan was empty, and there was no lasagna in the oven.

Sadie gasped. "Where's the lasagna." She gasped again. "But…where?"

The only sign that the lasagna had been there was a little bubbling sauce lining the thin crack between the door and the oven.

Sadie was shocked, but the expression on Rafe's face was pricelessly adorable.

She knew hers had to be just as comical as she quickly closed the door, expecting to find a gooey mess on the floor. But, no, there was no lasagna on the floor either. It had disappeared.

They stared at each other, totally baffled.

Rafe hiked a comical brow, then reached for the oven drawer and pulled it open.

And there in all its globby glory lay her lasagna in the bottom of the drawer.

Sadie's hand went to her chest, and she gasped. Then burst into laughter.

Rafe's shoulders were shaking, he was laughing

so hard and struggling to hold back. But once she started laughing, so he did too.

"The hot noodles just slid through both cracks!" Sadie giggled. She wasn't a giggler, but had to try to catch her breath as she wiped tears of laughter from her eyes.

"I don't know how, but that's what it did."

"It just went slurp," she mimicked the sound they'd heard and caused him to laugh more.

"What was that sound again?" he asked, his eyes glittering with mirth.

She giggled again. She never giggled, but she couldn't stop. She made the sound again, and he threw his head back and laughed heartily. And Sadie knew she would never, ever forget that moment.

"Dinner is ruined," she said.

He wrapped his arms around her and hugged her to him. "Forget about it," he growled, holding her close. "I'm taking you out to dinner tonight."

"But--"

"No buts. I'm going to clean this up, and then we're heading out after I grab a quick shower. It's the only thing to do after a sign like this. You worked hard on this meal, and then to have something this weird happen…it's a sign that I am surely supposed to take you out." He chuckled again, "That would probably never happen again even if we tried it."

"I have to agree. I'll clean it up."

"Nope. I will."

She looked around the kitchen. "Then I'll clean up the kitchen while you do that. Thank you."

He grinned. "I'm glad it happened. I've been wanting to take you out since the day you got here."

Sadie was not going to argue about it, not when she wanted to go out with him more than she'd ever wanted to go anywhere with anyone. She decided right then and there that lasagna was now her favorite food *not* to eat!

CHAPTER TWELVE

Two hours later, after Rafe had let the others know they'd have to grab dinner at Sam's or fix it themselves, he called ahead and ordered a to-go order from Sam's and picked it up at the back door. This was a date night for him and Sadie, and he wanted as few people as possible to know about it. Three people, to be exact. He knew Sam could keep a secret.

He wanted Sadie all to himself, and tonight he planned to have it that way.

"There are a lot of beautiful places on this ranch. The unique thing about Mule Hollow area is the landscape. We're not exactly hill country, but we're not exactly central Texas either. We have the best of both landscapes. Rocks and valleys and vistas, and yet we have oak trees that make artist's fingers itch to paint them. And in the spring, the bluebonnets are like carpets, they are so lush. I'm taking you to a great place for this…date."

Sadie smiled at him from her seat and didn't object to his using that word. "You love this place, don't you?"

He nodded. "I do. I find peace here." He drove through the pastures, glad they were almost to their destination.

"Peace. That sounds wonderful." She suddenly sounded a little down.

"Are you having second thoughts about calling off your wedding?" His stomach knotted as he looked at her. She shook her head, and relief surged through him. Parking the truck near a stand of trees, he covered her hand with his. "Then what's bothering you?"

She bit her lip and glanced out the window.

"Sadie?"

"I thought you wanted to show me a great place?"

His gut re-knotted. "Sure. Let's go. It's a short walk, but the payoff is worth it."

"As long as you have a flashlight to get me back, then I'm okay." She laughed.

"I have one. Nothing's going to happen to you on my watch." He glanced at her over his shoulder and wondered if that was what was bothering her. Or was it something more serious than a walk through the dark woods.

Sadie stared from the rocky cliff out over the river running rapidly about fifty feet below them. It was easy to see that and then on across the pastures as the sun began setting over the valley.

"This…makes me speechless." She glanced over at him and found him staring only at her. The turmoil churning in her stomach ramped up at the way he was studying her.

"You make me speechless," he said gently, his voice husky.

She groaned silently. The man could send rockets to the moon with those eyes of his. *Focus, Sadie. Focus.* "No wonder you find peace here," she said, softly, then forced her eyes back to view. The landscape, not the hot cowboy with the dreamy, dreamy eyes.

"Yeah, the views are fantastic. The people too. You fit right in." He tugged gently on a strand of hair hanging across her shoulder. "We…better eat before it gets cold."

"Good idea." She breathed a sigh of relief, since

she was having thoughts that involved getting lost in the woods for days with Rafe Masterson.

That was a really, really appealing idea.

He spun on his boots and strode toward the backpack, pulling out a blanket. Sadie helped get the blanket settled on a smooth spot of ground. Her pulse had gone from skittering to roaring like a wildfire in the last few seconds.

She knew her emotions were off. Knew she shouldn't trust them. Knew that the thoughts she was thinking were…emotionally overcharged because of everything that was going on in her head. But when he sank to that blanket and patted the spot beside him, she didn't hesitate. She sat on the blanket and forced herself to look back at the landscape. But nothing she did could stop the tingles that radiated through her as their shoulders brushed together, then stayed connected, as if magnetically attached.

As he handed her a plate and their fingers brushed, she shivered. "I know this is going to be great. Sam's an amazing cook," she babbled causing Rafe to chuckle.

"Yes, he is."

They ate in silence and watched the sunset as it began to change into an array of vivid oranges and pinks that seemed to accentuate the feelings filling her.

"Why don't you have a girlfriend?" It was obvious that he didn't have one, but she simply could not understand it. The man could have his pick, it seemed. And from what she'd heard Maddie casually mention, he hadn't dated anyone seriously at all. Hadn't had more than a few casual dates.

He stood and went over to a pile of limbs piled at the edge of the trees, pulled a few out and set them up to make a fire. She tucked her legs in front of her and wrapped her arms around them, resting her chin on her knees as she watched him, waiting for him to answer her question.

"I had a fiancée," he said, after he'd piled the branches into a pyramid and pulled a butane starter from his backpack to light some dried leaves and twigs.

When she couldn't stand waiting for him to continue any longer, she asked, "What happened?"

"I learned that she was only with me because I was doing well in the circuit. As soon as I messed up my knee, she was gone."

There was a tightness and an edge to his quietly spoken words. Sadie flinched inwardly at the blow that must have dealt him. Losing his career, his dream and his fiancée, the woman he loved, all at the same time. No wonder he was cautious or leery of dating. "She just left?" The question came out before she could stop it.

Finished getting the fire started, he rose from his crouched position and stared up at the moon that now hung brightly over the valley below them. Its glow reflected off the river. It looked like a gorgeous silver strand of ribbon deceptively peaceful looking, but she knew the river was powerful and turbulent. Much like Rafe's appearance at the moment. Though he looked calm and resigned, she sensed the deep hurt raging through him. She wanted to reach out to him. But she didn't.

She forced herself to remain seated and clutching her knees instead of him. How could this woman have done that to him?

He shrugged and came to settle back on the blanket beside her. "It was a little more complicated than that. In reality I knew it was coming. We'd started fighting all the time. She was disappointed that I didn't win the championship the year before. And I was disappointed that she didn't want to go ahead and get married and start a family. She didn't want a family right away."

141

"And you did."

He nodded. Sadie's heart clutched thinking how badly she wanted a family. And how often she'd talked with Andrew about it. Instead, he was focused--or so she'd thought--on his career.

"I did, and I do. But--" he looked straight at her with eyes that reflected the moon. "--I had my accident seven years ago, and I've never found anyone in all that time who inspired me to risk loving again."

Sadie couldn't look away. Her lungs burned with the need to breathe, but she couldn't.

He was saying, "Why are you looking at me like that?"

She knew in her heart of hearts that she was hoping, praying that the look in his eyes meant she had changed his outlook.

He threaded his fingers through her hair and cupped her head as he looked deeply into her eyes. "And then I met you. And you, from the very first moment, inspired me to hope again. Does that scare you?"

"A little." She had to be honest. Everything about Rafe turned her world upside down. "I've just made major changes in my life. This is all happening so fast. It hasn't even been a whole week."

"And yet I know that I want you in my life. I'm falling in love with you."

His words tumbled through her joyously. before she shut them down. "Rafe this is too fast." Her words were cut off when Rafe kissed her, took her breath away with a long, slow kiss.

She knew that without a doubt she'd made the right, if rash decision six days earlier. Because if she hadn't gone by her ex's condo to call off her wedding, then tomorrow she would have married the wrong man. For the wrong reason.

And she would have missed out on finding Rafe.

CHAPTER THIRTEEN

Sadie went through Saturday in a daze. She felt such relief knowing that she'd dodged the mistake of her life when she'd called off the wedding. There was no longer any trepidation or guilt about her decision. It had been right.

The dazed part was because of Rafe. In a matter of a short few days, he'd stolen her heart. Still, she tried to talk herself out of this notion.

Could she trust her heart after nearly messing up so badly with Andrew?

She made it through breakfast and was proud of the fact that all the food was edible. Everyone teased her and had a good laugh over the lasagna episode, and their chant became "Where's the lasagna" every time they saw her. It was funny, and she didn't mind being teased about it.

Rafe lingered in the kitchen before following

Chase, Dalton and Ty out to the trucks. "How are you doing today?"

"I'm okay," she said. "I know that calling the wedding off was the right move, and Amber saved me so much by canceling everything. So I'm fine."

"Good. I just wanted to make certain." He gave an encouraging smile that was so sexy that Sadie was still baffled by how this amazing man was still walking around single.

"We'll see you at lunch?"

She nodded. "And then I head over to No Place like Home for a bunny visit to the kids."

He surprised her with a sudden quick but hard kiss that sent her pulse skyrocketing. "You have a good heart, Sadie Archer. I love that about you." And then he strode out the door.

Sadie slumped against the stove as she watched him leave.

"Oh, my word…" she whispered. Could this really be happening?

Before she could move, Rafe strode back into the kitchen. His expression was almost fierce as he zeroed in and crossed the room to her.

Sadie's heart thundered, and her knees grew weak at the intensity of his gaze. He swept her into his arms.

"This is crazy, Sadie. But I just need you to know how I feel about this. Do you feel it too?"

She nodded, holding his gaze, but unable to speak because her mouth had gone parchment paper dry. But she did know what he was talking about and managed a stunned nod.

"Good," he said, a hint of a smile touching his lips, his eyes serious as they held hers. "Because I'm making myself clear right here and right now that I love you. And I hope that doesn't run you off, because I plan to do whatever it takes for as long as it takes to prove to you it's true. I want to win your heart. I want you in my life from here on out."

It really was happening. It really was. "I feel the same way. But...I need to take it slow."

He smiled. "We'll go as slow as you want. Just as long as you know I'm not a man to toy with your affections, let me tell you that I've never felt like this before. You're the best thing that has ever come into my life. Just so you know I aim to marry you, Sadie. If you'll have me." And then he kissed her.

"Wait," Sadie said, and pulled away. "Too fast. Way too fast."

Rafe pulled back and gave her a serious look that caused her heart to pound harder, if that were even possible. Then he tipped his hat. "Slow and easy from here on out. I just needed you to know how I felt. And, Sadie, I'm a one-woman man. You are all I'll ever want or need."

And then he strode out of the kitchen

Sadie had to sit in the nearest chair as her knees gave way.

Was this really happening? Could she let this happen?

Her heart suddenly felt heavy, and flashbacks of walking in and finding Andrew with another woman filled her mind.

She had never felt so low or used in all of her life.

Could she risk that again?

Could she?

Two hours later, still confused and worried about what was happening in her heart, Sadie had her bunny suit on, including her head with the floppy pink ears and her whiskered nose. She walked through the door of the beautiful large home that housed the refuge for abused women and their children, No Place Like Home.

"Here comes Flossy the Bunny," exclaimed Esther Mae, who was peeking around the doorway of a room where the children were all gathered.

Norma Sue stood at the other side of the arched entrance and was beaming as she gave Sadie a thumbs up as Sadie passed by her. Then she entered the room where the children were sitting cross-legged on the floor waiting.

"Hello. I'm Flossy, all right," she said with enthusiasm, her heart turning over as she took in each tiny face looking up at her. As it had been from the first moment she'd ever experienced this sensation, Sadie knew she was doing exactly what she was supposed to be doing. She loved the joy and wonder that exuded from the children. "I heard there were some boys and girls around here who wanted me to bring them some candy and read a couple of stories to them. Am I in the right place?"

"Yes!" They cried in unison.

Sadie's heart melted as she took the pink sack she carried over her shoulder and set it on the floor and she sank into the waiting chair. Adela stood nearby.

"Well, then, let's see what we have." She grinned inside the big head, knowing that her bunny face had a huge smile on it already. Sometimes she wished the kids could see how much joy their faces actually gave her. She pulled out lollipops and a small sack of homemade goodies that the Matchmakin' Posse had fixed up for the ten children at her feet. The matchmakers did more for this community than fix up couples. They had huge hearts, and it was easy to see that as they helped her pass out the bags.

Dottie and the mothers sat in chairs behind the kids, and Sadie had to block out her sadness from looking at the fading bruises on two of the women's faces. Thankfully none of the children had bruises, at least not visible ones. She knew, though, that more than likely their little hearts were in turmoil from the experiences they'd been through. Pushing that out of her thoughts, she pulled out the first story.

"Y'all ready for a story?"

A little girl took the treat Adela held out to her and came over to Sadie. The child stared up into her face and kissed her bunny cheek. Sadie's heart melted.

"Thank you," she whispered in Sadie's big ear, then turned and hurried to her seat.

"You have big feet," said a little boy sitting in the front row. He was eating his lollipop.

"They help me hop a long way." Sadie smiled, and opened the book and began to read. She'd read the story so much over the last few months that she almost knew it by heart. When she was done, she gave the children time to ask questions. After they were done, she let the ladies lead them into the dining room and kitchen area where they had refreshments and a cute photo area. Sadie took a photo with each child. One little girl, with dark hair and big navy eyes, watched her intently for most of the time. Finally, when her came to get her picture, she came over and climbed up into Sadie's lap and gave her a kiss on her fuzzy cheek. Sadie's heart turned to mush right there.

When it was time to leave after many hugs and waves and the promise to return, she headed out the door. Before she got to her car, a young woman came from inside and stopped her. She had a fading bruise on her cheek.

"Thank you," she called. "Olivia, the shy little girl who kissed you? That's my daughter. She, she hasn't talked much since I took her and left her daddy."

"I'm so sorry. I noticed how cautious she was. It's probably understandable, given the situation you must have been in. I find you very brave."

"I don't feel brave. I feel like such a failure."

Sadie thought about how she'd been feeling

with the whole Andrew fiasco. "You know, I recently called off my own wedding and ran. And if I let myself dwell on that, I'd feel the same way. But I'm not going to let myself do that. I thank God that my eyes were opened before I got myself into the bad situation. I'm thankful for you and for the sake of your little girl that your eyes have been opened and you got out of your situation before you were hurt anymore or Olivia was hurt anymore." Sadie took off her bunny head so the woman could see her. "You are not a failure, and neither am I. We're two women who have to take the first steps of the rest of our lives. What's your name?"

"Beverly."

"It's nice to meet you, Beverly. We are taking the first steps of the rest of our lives together. And we have a whole new bright future ahead of us. I think that makes us successes. We're in control of where we go from here."

"Thank you." Beverly smiled cautiously. "You're right."

Sadie reached out and placed her paw on Beverly's arm. "I'm staying at the New Horizon ranch. Dottie has my number. If you want to have lunch or coffee one day, call me. I'd love to visit."

Beverly's eyes grew misty, and she nodded.

"I mean it, Beverly. You are not alone here. One thing I've found out about Mule Hollow is that it's a welcoming, generous place. And I want to be a part of that generosity. I'd love to take you to lunch and be your friend."

"Okay. I'll call."

Sadie couldn't help herself. She hugged the woman. And then she rolled up her eighteen inch feet, squeezed her large bunny rump into her car and drove back to New Horizon Ranch. And she was smiling all the way.

She wasn't going to let herself be held back by fear any longer.

CHAPTER FOURTEEN

She drove into the yard to find a shiny red Corvette sitting in the drive. Her heart sank. There sat Andrew at the patio table, looking out of place in his business suit and tie. "What are you doing here?"

He crossed the patio to her, a frown on his face. "I came to explain. To fix this."

Sadie stared at him. "Explain what? There is no way you can explain yourself out of the situation that involved you locked in an embrace, kissing Adriana like there was no tomorrow."

"It was nothing. It just happened. It didn't mean anything."

"Whoa, just hold on a minute." Sadie almost laughed this was so ridiculous. "Telling me it meant nothing is not helping your situation. Telling you are sorry and you made a horrible mistake would be the better thing to say. But even that wouldn't help this situation or make a difference."

"It was a horrible mistake. And I am sorry. I never meant to hurt you. It-it just got out of hand. It won't happen again." He reached out and wrapped his hand around her arm, stepping closer. "I love you, Sadie."

Sadie shook her head. Looking up at him, she felt nothing but regret that she'd thought he was the man for her. What came to mind was Rafe , strong, steadfast and so caring. "No. No, you don't." She started to step away, but Andrew's grip tightened. "Sadie, it was just a mistake--"

"Let go of the lady," Rafe said, drawing both Sadie and Andrew to look at him. He had come from the barn and was standing about fifty feet away. His hat was low on his forehead, but even in the shadow, there was no denying the danger in his eyes.

"She's my fiancée. Who are you?" Andrew snapped, and Sadie knew this wasn't going to be good.

"I'm not your fiancée. I called the wedding off. Let me go."

"You heard Sadie. Let her go."

Andrew looked at her, anger glinting in his gaze.

"Is this the reason you've been hiding out here? This cowboy--"

Sadie yanked her arm free and stepped back. "This cowboy found me when I needed help and helped me. But you know what? He is one of the reasons I'm hiding out here. He gave me a place to get over the shock of finding you with your secretary the week before our wedding."

Rafe had crossed to stand just behind her, so near she could feel his warmth.

"I think now would be a good time for you to leave," Rafe said, warning in his tone.

Andrew glared from him to her.

Sadie had to smile. "Goodbye, Andrew."

His eyes narrowed briefly, but then he strode away, his shoulders stiff beneath his suit jacket. After he'd gotten into his car, shot them a glare, and driven off, Sadie turned to Rafe. They were standing very close, and he didn't step away, which was just the way Sadie wanted it.

"What could I have been thinking?"

"About what?"

"When I thought Andrew was the man for me."

Rafe's brows met. "I was wondering that same thing."

She hid her smile. "I bet you were. Rafe, I can't

believe this has happened, but I can't deny it any longer. I love you, Rafe."

He pulled her slowly into his embrace. "And I love you with all my heart, Sadie." And then he kissed her. His arms tightened around her, and she never wanted him to let her go. "Will you marry me?" he asked.

A thrill raced through her. "That sounds like heaven to me. I love you so," she murmured against his lips. And she knew she was going to have to work very hard to take it slow as she'd said that morning. And then her mind went blank, and all she could think about was the man holding her and kissing her with all the promise of the future to come.

She knew this time there would be no hesitations. This was right. This was the man of her dreams.

Dear Reader,

Thank you so much for reading RAFE book 2 in my New Horizon Ranch of Mule Hollow book series! If you haven't yet read book 1 HER TEXAS COWBOY, it's Maddie and Cliff's story, Rafe's twin brother, and is available in ebook and print also. Y'all asked for more Mule Hollow and I've had fun giving that to you with these new books! If you enjoyed RAFE, I hope you will recommend it to your friends. Maybe write a review on the retail site where you purchased it, or talk about it on Facebook or Goodreads, and let people know. It really helps me reach others with my stories by getting the word out!

Happy Reading! And all my best to you!
Debra Clopton

More Books by **Debra Clopton**

For the complete list, visit her website
www.debraclopton.com

61644213R00092

Made in the USA
Lexington, KY
16 March 2017